I0527070

THEOCLEA
(The Delphic Oracle)
and
PYTHAGORAS
IN
EGYPT

Second Edition

PanOrpheus

PanOrpheus Press
Thorndale, Pa. 19372
Theoclea (The Delphic Oracle)
And Pythagoras
In Egypt

ISBN: 0615502261
ISBN-13: 9780615502267

The Fingerprint

She left a fingerprint
on the Gate
It took so long to get so near
Now YOU are here,
Why hesitate?
For most of us the path is clear
Now why stand still when you've come so far?
Your strength and will
Tell us who you are

Ah, yes this Gate may be your last,
and you are filled with fear, of course
GO THROUGH!
The stones have all been cast,
this Gate will lead you to the Source!

…from
Thirty Days of Meditation and
Group Workings
Using the KeyRose
PanOrpheus (2011)

Thanks and Appreciation

Special thanks go out to all of the people at Four Quarters-particularly Karynna, for giving me the character of Miriam, Sophia for the talks that we had about Egypt, and Rosanna, for being Theoclea at the Ecumenicon 2010, and giving me insight into Theoclea. More thanks go to Talitha, for playing Theoclea in one of my workshops, and giving me the inspiration to do the 'Aletheia' ritual-a ritual that we co-wrote that helped me to break out, and have Sonja and Aura appear in a ritual drama. See the 'Whispers' book for Talitha's brilliant take on the Triumph of the Oracle Alethia ca. 279 B.C. Without the sensitive work that the women above put into their portrayals of Theoclea, I would have been at a loss in the writing of certain scenes in this book. The Oracles were amazing women, some of the most powerful and gifted women of all time. There is not nearly enough credit or attention given to their unique place in human history.

Also thanks to Irene of the Barajagala Bellydance Troupe for being Aura, (www.btribalbellydance.com.) and Megan for being Sonja, the singer, musician, and master of the crystal wand in the ritual drama. Even though those characters make a brief appearance in this book-they are important to me in the scheme of things.

Thanks to Schuyler and Kharma of the 'Ohio Burn Unit' for suggestions on the fire entertainment. Their web address is www.ohioburnunit.com. Alan Shear presented me with the idea for the 'Tribal Council', and the use of images, archetypes and role playing in one of Theoclea's visions. Thanks be to you, Alan. This will be examined more closely in a short story, 'The Reunion-Reflections, Interventions, and Transitions' in a book of short stories that will be out in 2011, called 'Phoebe (The Delphic Oracle) meets Dracula (The Vampire)', and other stories...by Panorpheus.

Celtic Myth and Moonlight is where it all started. Thanks go to Dottie, the owner of Celtic Myth, for all of your encouragement. I'd also like to thank Chuck Wolf, author of the book 'Neesa', for his encouragement and patience in listening and sharing ideas about book publishing. Thanks go to P.J. and Reagan, and their mom, Mikki, for giving me the inspiration for 'The Star Children', Abderus and Alcena, and members of the Pennypack group for their support. P.J. and Reagan are young people- in their teens.

Thanks also go to members of the 'Assembly of the Wheel'. Special thanks must go to Jim Welch for his seminar on Ethics-the eight points of Theoclea's speech are a direct outgrowth of Jim Welch's Seminar and the work of Assembly elders like Ivo, Michael and others in considering what I see as a modern set of ethical principles. The Crystal Castings in this book are fictitious. Read Ivo Dominguez book-'Castings: The Creation of Sacred space (Wheel of Trees)' for the real thing.

Thanks to Amy and Bess for showing me what a Priestess of Apollo and a Priestess of Dionysus would do and say, and Charles of the 'Ecumenicon' for his continued support.

I must mention Lois (Iszabella) and her "Gypsy' dancers. Check out Lois' website at www.NewWorldGypsy. com. Many people have seen you and your troupe at Pennsylvania's 'Renaissance Faire'. I based the beginning of the 'Parade' chapter on your dancers.

Special Thanks go to 'the Holders of the KeyRose', people who have taken my classes and use the KeyRose.

I also must thank the Independent Egyptologist John Anthony West for his book 'Serpent in the Sky', and the DVD 'The Mystery of the Sphinx'. The ideas about the age and possible origin of the Sphinx, as well as a theoretical history of the Sphinx can be found in the pages of his book and video. Thanks also go to Mr. West for making me aware of the contributions of R.A.Schwaller de Lubicz to the understanding of Egyptian Architecture, and their number system. I must also mention the work of Dr. Robert Schoch, a Geologist whose work on the age of the Sphinx is featured in the documentary mentioned above.

The theory of an internal ramp inside of the Great Pyramid of Giza has been offered by Jean-Pierre Houdin, a French Architect in the National Geographic DVD video "Unlocking the Secrets of the Great Pyramid".

My apologies to others that I haven't mentioned here...

PanOrpheus-Winter, 2011

Synopsis of the other two Theoclea books...

Below you will find a synopsis of Theoclea (The Delphic Oracle) in Eleusis, as well as a synopsis of Theoclea (The Delphic Oracle) sees Atlantis, two other books in the series.

After the synopsis, you will find a list of the main characters, symbols, divination tools, medallions, and other items of importance in the two other books. I suggest that you refer to the list before reading chapter one.

Theoclea (The Delphic Oracle) in Eleusis

The setting is Delphi, Greece ca. 500 B.C. We meet Theoclea as a child, and share her experience of her first vision. During the vision she saves the lives of her friends, Troyana and Anka, and she sees the future for the first time. We then meet them as adults-Theoclea has become the Delphic Oracle, Troyana has become The Sybil, a card reader, and Anka has become the Queen of Hydros, and an expert in using stones for divination.

All of the events in the book lead up to a speech that Theoclea has decided to deliver to the Pilgrims before they attend the Mysteries of Eleusis. Theoclea is protected by her Guardian/Protector, Panelle, and her Counselor, Morain, an empath. We also meet Vorios, the chief magician of the Temple of Delphi, and Pythagoras, a priest and mathematician/scientist. The Keyrose divination tool is shown for the first time. Bella, a dancer is presented, and we see her and her troupe perform in the tent city at Eleusis prior to the Mysteries. Finally Theoclea delivers 'The Great Speech at Eleusis'.

The speech is tinged with magic and portents of the future. Finally, Theoclea touches the first Gate, and sees The Guardian.

Theoclea (The Delphic Oracle) sees Atlantis

Theoclea has a disturbing dream of destruction, and seeks the advice of her friends and advisors. A festival is being planned that will include two rituals of transformation. We meet the children of Pythagoras and

Theoclea, a boy and a girl-Abderus and Alcena. There are workshops, vendors, the raising of a huge stone, and other events. The festival is interrupted by the appearance of Davros, a descendant of 'The Sons of Belial', warriors of Atlantis. Through the use of magic, Theoclea and her friends defeat Davros and his army. Theoclea then goes on to have a vision of Atlantis, where we meet Axcelotl, the Queen of Atlantis, her guardian Sonja, and her counselor, Aura. Axcelotl is the leader of 'The Crystal Ones', the keepers of 'The Crystal Power' that is crucial to the residents of Atlantis and its' outposts. Through dream and vision, Theoclea, Morain, Panelle, Pythagoras, and Vorios journey backward in time to the days before the destruction of Atlantis. We also meet Vorios' brother, Hermeticus, and The Grandfather. The Grandfather is the leader of 'The Children of the Law of One' the peaceful, spiritual people of Atlantis. After The Grandfather dispenses his wisdom, Theoclea meets Aurora, another of 'the Children of the Law of one', and finally ends up on the edge of a cliff overlooking the doomed capital city of Atlantis. She meets the Dancer, who gives her the gift of being a healer, meets the Guardian, touches the second Gate, and sees the destruction of Atlantis.

The characters and Symbols...

I feel that it's necessary for me to give you the background on some of the symbols and objects that will appear in the story.

Theoclea.... Theoclea was the first Oracle to become a Priestess of Apollo, (The Light) and Dionysus (The Dark), although we know, dear reader that it is not as simple as that, and appearances can be deceiving. In fact, as you may already know, Theoclea possessed the Rose Medallion, the Token of Inanna, and considered herself to be a Priestess of Inanna as well...balancing the two Gods.

Pythagoras... Educated in Egypt for eleven years, Pythagoras was taught mathematics, rudimentary geometry, magic, and many other useful subjects. He was one of the few Greek Priests to be educated in Egypt.

He had to leave Egypt when the Persians attacked the country, and ended the reign of the Pharaohs. After spending some time in Babylon, he was invited to return home to Greece and become one of the teachers of the next Delphic Oracle-Theoclea. He served as the High Priest at her Initiation Ceremony. During her initiation ceremony, the 'Great Rite' may have been celebrated privately by Pythagoras and Theoclea. He left three days after her initiation, and nine months later, twins were born. There was great excitement about this in the Temple. A child had not been born of the initiation rite for 700 years and their birth of twins was seen as a good omen by the residents of the Temple.

The Star Children, Alcena and Abderus..... The children were not told who their parents were until they were about thirteen years of age. That was done for their protection, of course. They were raised with the other orphans who had been taken in by the Temple. They are now about 15 years old.

The Symbols....

The Keys... The keys showed where a person was in their spiritual development. If you had the **Gold key**, you were a follower of Apollo, and used the key to enter the altar room of Apollo, where you studied the highest philosophy, the highest thoughts of humankind. It has been said that children are born with the gold key.

There were many people who were born with the gold key, then it was taken away from by them by life itself, and they were given the **Black Key and a Wound.** With the black key they could only enter the altar room of Dionysus, and experience the dark side of life, the midnight revels, the fruit of the vine...things that when taken to the lower levels without moderation can ultimately lead to a fall into the Abyss.

When the wound healed, one could be given the **Red Key**, after sufficient study and experience. The red Key could only be given by someone who had achieved the highest spiritual status-like The Oracle. It was the key to all of the altar rooms of all of the religions, past, present, and future.

The Rose Medallion or Token of Inanna...
The Rose medallion described in this book was supposedly made by an artisan in Sumer at the height of the worship of Inanna. If one were to look at the face side of the medallion, the face of Inanna, and then turn it over to the blank side, wonders could be seen and heard, but only by those who had the gifts to be receptive to its revelations. The artisan may have been a reincarnation of 'The grandfather', the leader of The Children of the

Law of One, on Atlantis, prior to its' destruction in 9600 BC. He may have made three medallions at that time, and they are described as the story progresses.

Vorios... The Chief magician of the Temple of Delphi, Vorios is an immortal. He was one of the sons of 'The Grandfather' on Atlantis.

Morain... Theoclea's Counselor, an empath who can send out waves of emotion and empathy to one or two people, or a large crowd. She can meld minds with Theoclea, if Theoclea allows it, and in doing so, see part or all of Theoclea's visions, and more.

Panelle... Theoclea's Counselor/Protector. She had the responsibility to protect Theoclea with her wards and spells, and had other magical powers as well.

The Oracles-

Gaia... The first to hold The Seat of Prophecy at the temple of Delphi, during an indeterminate period before the temple became the Temple of Apollo. It has been said that Delphi was the seat of a matriarchal goddess-centered religion in the distant past, possibly during the time of the Titans. Gaia's name meant 'The Earth', of course, and sometime after her death she was given the title and responsibilities of a Goddess.

Themis... The second to hold The Seat of Prophecy at the Temple of Delphi, after Gaia. Her name meant 'Tradition' and she was considered to represent Justice as well.

Phoebe... The third to hold the Seat of Prophecy, after Themis. Her name meant 'the bright and shining one'.

The Spirits of Eternal Vigilance... They originally lived on our plane during and prior to the destruction of Atlantis. After their demise, they became spirits who could be seen as amorphous lights on our plane, and they had the power to become recognizable to us in their original forms if they chose to.

Sonja... Sonja was usually dressed in gold, and was the master of the crystal wand. She was also a fine singer, and could control the wand in many ways, often with just one exquisite musical tone.

Aura... Aura usually dressed in black, and was a dancer. She was mute, and communicated with delicate hand gestures, dance moves, and mental images that she sent out telepathically. She was also an empath, like Morain, and could send out waves of emotion and empathy to one person, or a crowd.

Axcelotl... Axcelotl was the last Queen of Atlantis, before the destruction, and a leader of 'The crystal ones', those who held the secret of the crystal power. After her demise on our plane, she became the leader of the Spirits of Eternal Vigilance, and possessed the ultimate healing powers.

The Grandfather... The leader of the 'Children of the Law of one', the peaceful group that resided on Atlantis before the destruction. He was the maker of the first three Atlantean medallions, and in a later incarnation in Sumer, he made the Rose Medallion.

Contents

Take a look at our new website
www.panorpheus.com.

Our books are also listed on:
www.amazon.com
www.lulu.com,
www.barnesandnoble.com and other fine book sites.

Search 'books'-PanOrpheus, Theoclea, or Phoebe, KeyRose, Oracle, and other search words, and some of our titles come up.

You can contact me at Facebook under the name of Pan Orpheus.
There is also a 'Delphic Oracle mystical magical fact and fiction' group on Facebook that I have started.

Foreword

We have finally come to what I've been calling the 'Egypt' book of the Theoclea series. I've been telling people all along that a good mystery reveals its' secrets in the last six pages, and this book is no exception. Many people have asked me why I've used the image of the 'the old projector and its' frozen piece of black and white film' to start all of the visions that have occurred in the other books. This book reveals that it is a key piece in the puzzle. That said, I will say no more, I don't want to spoil it for you.

The Greece and Egypt of these books is an alternate reality, not historical, although there is ample history here-enough to make you get comfortable and think that you are in ancient Greece or Egypt. Modern Cairo did not exist as a city at the time of the visit ca. 520 B.C. of Theoclea and her entourage.

Thebes and the Temple of Luxor did exist, but Thebes was not always the capital city of Egypt. There were Pharaohs, Ikhnaton, (or Akhenaton) for instance, who moved entire populations to newly built cities that were to be the new capital of Egypt. The fact remains that for most of Egypt's history it was one of the richest nations on Earth, with seemingly limitless reserves of gold, and priceless treasures.

The Pharaohs and other leaders could easily set up new capital cities if they wanted to.

As the author of these works I must say that it has been my intention all along to introduce new perspectives, new ways of looking at things, and Theoclea and her friends have been the perfect characters for doing this. I have drawn from a variety of religious and mystical thought. It has been my intention, that while entertaining you, I have tried to pose one 'mystery' after another, to show you that there is a constant randomness in the flow of time from one moment to another, with a multitude of possibilities each step of the way. The poetic, 'mythos' approach yields more than a string of dubious facts, and Theoclea's gifts do not lend themselves to a 'logos' interpretation. There are frames within frames within frames here, an almost 'fractal' quality, if I can borrow the word from the new geometry of our time.

The reader will be rewarded by trying to figure out why certain names were chosen. 'Carl' the facilitator briefly appears in a vision. 'Sonja' and 'Aura' are the spirits of eternal vigilance at a key dramatic moment. Certain phrases ring in my mind, and if Theoclea mentions that "I hope that you find beauty in my words... I have a certain attitude on these matters"-dear reader I assure you that all of her words have been chosen carefully.

In this book, also, Pythagoras and 'The Star Children' have come to the fore. You'll be reading more about the adventures of Abderus and Alcena in the future. I hope that I have captured more of the essence of Pythagoras, and revealed to you why he was an extraordinary teacher and thinker.

In the end though, it is Theoclea who captures our hearts once more- faced with the possibility of having seen her own death, and the instrument of death in a vision- she steadfastly continues on her chosen path, a path that started, as she reveals, with finding the Pan statue and the Treasure chest as a child, playing with her friends-in chapter one of 'Theoclea (The Delphic Oracle) in Eleusis.'

Blessed Be, Theoclea.

PanOrpheus, 2011

Chapter One... Pythagoras and Vorios talk

"Pythagoras, are you enjoying your stay here at Delphi?" Vorios said. They were outside in a half circle of standing stones that stood next to the Temple. It was a sunny day and there were no clouds to block the sun. A few crows flew across the sun, landed on one of the stones, then watched and listened, as crows often do.

"Well, it's been almost nine months since our adventure in Atlantis, Vorios, and I see that not much has changed since I left. I'll be here for perhaps four months this time, and I'm teaching at the orphan's school. I've gotten to know Abderus and Alcena better- until last year, I didn't even know that I was the father of twins.

1

I'd been away from Delphi for almost thirteen years and Theoclea didn't feel that there was a reason for me to know about the children. She didn't even want you, Vorios, to tell me about them, even though she knew that we met occasionally. Her decision was based on the welfare of the children, and she thought that it would have been a danger to them if word got out that they were the children of Pythagoras and Theoclea. We had a hint of that with the Davros situation, a descendant of 'The Sons of Belial' trying to attack the Temple with his troops!" Vorios nodded in agreement.

"Pythagoras, I asked you to meet me here, because there are things that we must discuss. I'm an immortal-I don't change, even though I've been different people at various times, a politician, a warrior, a mystic. I've also taken different names at different times. I don't age. We've all had our adventures together. We've all been to Atlantis, and I've grieved for many months over the deaths of my father-The Grandfather, and Hermeticus, my brother, the magician. Axcelotl and Aurora must have also died in the destruction of Atlantis. The grieving has ended, and I have something here that Hermeticus wanted you to have, Pythagoras. I've kept it with me all this time, waiting for the right moment." He carried a large pouch with him.

"On my last night in Atlantis, I stayed in my brother's tent. He had a leather bag, and brought out the medallion that he owned, the one with the man surrounded by the triangles. He wanted me to give it to you, Pythagoras. He interpreted the three flashes that were aimed at you, from the medallion, as a sign that the medallion was now to be given to you." Vorios then reached into the pouch, and took the medallion out. The face side showed the man's face with triangles surrounding it.

Pythagoras stared at it in disbelief, as Vorios continued-

"Three medallions were made by The Grandfather, my father. We will now have two with the male faces, and Theoclea has the Rose Medallion that was made thousands of years after the deaths of my father-'The Grandfather', my brother, Hermeticus, and the others, Aurora, and Axcelotl."

"It may be that the Grandfather was reincarnated in Sumer at the height of the worship of Inanna. If that was the case, it would explain why Theoclea's medallion works as well as the earlier ones. Even the red clay is exactly the same. It must have come from some island that was originally part of Atlantis. The last medallion that the Grandfather made on Atlantis was the one that

Axcelotl, the Queen of Atlantis wore. It had her face on it and a crown of interlocking crystals. It was probably destroyed in the catastrophic destruction of Atlantis, and lies with Axcelotl in a watery grave. She never left Atlantis. Neither did my brother, or the Grandfather, or Aurora."

"There's one more thing, Pythagoras, after Hermeticus gave me the medallion in his tent, to give to you, he said that there was a book that he wanted to show me. There were originally two volumes, but one had been stolen. He wanted me to take the book back to our time, so that you and I, Pythagoras, could study it. My brother and I discussed the book all night, and had the sense that it was useless without the other volume. He told me what he knew about the process described in the book, but the information was incomplete. He seemed to feel that the medallions would be helpful in this regard. Later, we went over to the Grandfather's tent. I had to leave and wanted to say my last goodbyes to my father and brother. The Grandfather told me that he had seen the immediate future...that the Continent of Atlantis would be destroyed completely within the week. He had tried to convince Axcelotl to give him her medallion, to give to me, but she said that if the prediction was right, then the medallion with her face and crown of crystals on it should die with her."

"If that happened, Pythagoras, then the medallions will never be together in any one place. They may never be together again as they were in Axcelotl's Temple. Any indication that you and I ever have that Axelotl's medallion survived the destruction and her death, would be a magical synchronicity of immense importance."

"My brother, The Grandfather and I said our good-byes, shed some tears, and hugged each other. It was a scene that I shall never forget. I then walked out of the Grandfather's tent, walked ahead into a white fog, with the medallion and the book, and knew that I had seen Atlantis for the last time."

"So, Pythagoras-that's the story. I've held this medallion for almost nine months-as always, waiting for the right moment. Pythagoras, I present you with the medallion of my brother, Hermeticus, who died in that horrific catastrophe on Atlantis, 9000 years ago." He handed the medallion to Pythagoras. Pythagoras held it, and there were tears in his eyes. He touched the triangles, and the face, then looked at Vorios, and said-

"You may have lost a brother in Atlantis, but you have become like a brother to me, and now that we have two of the medallions, our bond has increased.

They embraced each other. Vorios then reached into the pouch and took out a book. It was bound in an unknown material that had a shimmering crystalline quality to it. "This is the book that my brother gave to me. The second volume is lost. He wanted both of us to read it." Vorios handed the book to Pythagoras. The title was in gold leaf and it said:

The Key to the Crystal Power
Vol. I

Vorios and Pythagoras spent the night looking at the book and talking about it, and by the time that morning came, Pythagoras had made a decision.

"Vorios, there is only one man that I know who would have any idea of where the second volume may have been hidden, or what it might have contained. To meet him, we must travel to Egypt. I mean that we must all travel to Egypt, Theoclea, you, the children, Morain, Panelle, and perhaps others as well."

"Theoclea once mentioned to me her desire to deliver a speech in Egypt. If we all go there, we may be able to solve the mystery of what happened to the second book. The man that I'm thinking of was one of my teachers during the eleven years that I spent studying to be a Priest. Even at that time his sight was failing. He was called-'The Scribe'."

Pythagoras looked down, as if the mere mention of the name evoked an onslaught of memories. There was silence between them for perhaps a minute.

"The Scribe, I know of him," Vorios replied.

"Vorios, I thought that you told me that you've never been to Egypt," Pythagoras said.

"When you send a message to The Scribe, mention my name, see if he remembers..." Vorios said.

"Vorios, you're being very mysterious about this, but I'll do as you say."

Vorios squinted up at the sun.

"Pythagoras, what time is it?"

Pythagoras looked at the stones, and then at the Sun.

"It's noon."

"Yes, it's noon," Vorios said. "There is a place that I go to, around noon each say. There is a column there that may be more than thirty feet high. I take a blanket and a cushion, and arrange them so that when I sit down, the sun seems to be balanced at the top of the column. In this way, I can follow the course of the sun throughout the year. The blanket and cushion are placed in a slightly different spot each day, I like feeling the sunlight on my face."

He started to walk away from Pythagoras, then turned, and said, "You're going to have to learn the secrets of The Scribe from him." He walked a few more paces, then stopped, turned once more, faced Pythagoras, and said, "The Scribe is…" he looked at the ground and then at Pythagoras. There were tears in his eyes. "The Scribe' is…very old."

With that, Vorios walked away, leaving Pythagoras to ponder what had happened. The crows flew up and crossed the sun.

That day, Pythagoras spoke to Theoclea, and she mentioned once again that for a long time, she had been feeling the desire to travel to Egypt, and speak to the Egyptian people. She even had visions of it, and saw herself standing on a platform between the Paws of the Sphinx. She insisted that Morain, Panelle, the children, Abderus and Alcena, and others, would accompany them. Theoclea then gave him some bottles of a liquid, and oils that might help to improve the Scribe's eyesight and memory.

"Oh yes, Pythagoras, and there is an old friend of mine, Skyfire, the head of a fire entertainment troupe based in Cairo. He visits me occasionally. I'd like to send a personal letter to him, telling him about the possibility of our trip. Also, I want to take some gifts for the Royal Court, and gifts for Skyfire and others. Do we still have those fine wines down in the cellar of the Temple? I'd like to make sure that he is sent a few bottles of our finest wine before we set out on the trip. If I remember correctly, he enjoys wine!"

"Skyfire, I've heard of him, Theoclea, he's a well-known fire entertainer!"

"I know," said Theoclea. "Do you know that two members of his troupe are athletes from Greece? Skyfire himself was born in Greece!"

"I learn things from you every day, Theoclea"

Pythagoras wrote a message to the Scribe, telling him that it was his intention to return to Egypt, with Theoclea, He included Theoclea's liquid, and the oils, and instructions on how to use them with the message. Morain, Panelle, the children, Abderus and Alcena, and others, would accompany them. He mentioned the book, but was vague about the reason that they all had to go, saying something like 'Theoclea feels the need to see Egypt, speak to the Egyptian people, and become acquainted with Egyptian Culture'. She also wanted The Scribe to try the liquid in the bottles that she was sending, and to try the oils under his eyes.

9

He also started to work on a letter to the Royal Court of Egypt. In the message to the Court, he emphasized, first and foremost, that Theoclea had mentioned a desire to give a speech in a special setting. It would be a major speech, comparable to her speech at Eleusis, but containing a lifetime of her thoughts and observations.

He emphasized that Theoclea had visions of the speech taking place between the Paws of the Sphinx. Of course, he did not mention the book.

Chapter Two... The message from The Scribe.

Pythagoras met with Vorios three weeks later. Surprisingly, it took only a few weeks for messages to travel to Egypt and back. They met in Vorios' chambers.

"I've talked to Theoclea, Morain and Panelle about traveling to Egypt, and Theoclea was very excited, although Morain and Panelle looked worried. Theoclea assured them that everything would be alright. She's very excited about taking the trip. She definitely wants to give a speech while we are there, and has had visions of this. As a matter of fact, she told me that she has been working on the speech for a long time, and feels that it would be appropriate to give it while standing between the paws of the great statue, 'The Sphinx'. The speech itself will provide an excellent reason for our trip. I've sent messages about this to Egypt, and have already

11

received an invitation from the people that I still know who are in the Royal Court. Many of them remember me. The message from the Royal Court reveals a great excitement about the visit of Theoclea, the children and the others in our entourage."

"I'm going to suggest that we all make arrangements to leave for Egypt as soon as possible. Morain and Panelle, of course, will have to come along to be with Theoclea. We've agreed to take the 'Star Children' along too-Alcena and Abderus. Have I told you? During the past six months, Theoclea told them that we are their parents! They've known this for some time now, and the Egyptians are anxious for the children of Pythagoras and Theoclea to meet their children"

Vorios smiled. "Yes, they are old enough now to understand. We'll take the KeyRose box, the three medallions and the Keys along. I know the Egyptians, and they'll want Theoclea to show them all of her divination tools. You and I will certainly be asked about the Philosophy of the Keys, and other matters of Magic and Science."

"Vorios-there was another message that a received from Egypt-a reply from The Scribe."

"Here it is"-Pythagoras handed Vorios a scroll-

12

"Pythagoras, I was delighted to hear from you. Yes, of course I remember you! You were my finest student! I am blind now, but I hear occasionally about your accomplishments. The other scribes read to me every day. We are not unsophisticated, you know, and we get news from all over. We know about Theoclea-her book 'Whispers' has been read to me. You were one of her teachers, and I recognize some of you in that book. Her great speech at Eleusis has been read to me as well. I would have liked to have been there to hear her, and to have seen the Magic that accompanied the speech. Where did it come from?"

"With your message you sent some bottles of a liquid that Theoclea says could improve my eyesight. I'm willing to try anything to restore my eyesight and memory, and will drink the prescribed amount each day-also thank her for the oils-I will use them every day as well. I'm also very excited at the prospect of hearing her speak."

"I have always been called The Scribe. I don't remember the names that I used in other incarnations. I am old now and blindness and forgetfulness have overtaken me. Blindness has been a sign of the end of all of my past lives, and I remember some of them in great detail. Others seem to be almost forgotten. I was there when my friend, the architect, Hemiunu built the Great Pyramid at Giza, during the Time of Khufu. That was almost 2000 years ago.

"I copied his architectural writings, plans, and diagrams and made them into books for him. I believe that he said that he buried the books in the Pyramid, perhaps somewhere along a mile-long internal ramp yet to be discovered. I remember him crawling through hidden entrances all over the pyramid to make sure that no cracks were appearing in the inner chambers. He was a man who demanded perfection, and personally inspected the work as it went along."

"I remember the activity each day. It was very exciting. Large stones being lifted and put on the trolley that rolled along the Grand Gallery-with heavy counterweights on the other side. I remember the sound of the log rollers as the great slabs were pulled along tracks in the Grand Gallery. There seemed to be hundreds of men involved in the project, and they were not slaves, for they were paid for their work, and returned to their farms during the inundations and at other times during the year. At the height of the activity a number of new stones were put in place every day! The men lived near the site when the work was going on. I believe that there was also an outside ramp that was also used."

"Hemiunu's books were not put in the King's Chamber, or the Queen's chamber. Even he was afraid of tomb robbers, and he told me that he hid them in a chamber off of the internal ramp. I remember that blocks and cranes were used to lift the

14

blocks, and that the corners were open to allow this to be done. That was an exciting time."

"In some of my incarnations, I have been a teacher, scholar, scribe, craftsman, or artisan of some kind. I remember being in Sumer during the time of the worship of Inanna. I was an artisan during that time, a maker of fine jewelry, medallions and the like. I remember making medallions from a special red clay. They were probably made for someone in the Royal family. Maybe my memory deceives me-you must forgive an old man-I am blind and I am probably imagining things. With each day my memories recede. I have no memories of incarnations during the last 2000 years, since I was there with Hemiunu."

"I seem to also remember being an artisan on Atlantis, during the last days. I seem to remember making medallions and jewelry. Sometimes in my dreams, I hear voices and whispers. I also remember an incarnation of perhaps as much as eight thousand years ago. I was a sculptor, and lived near The Nile. At that time there were natural, huge rock formations along the Nile called 'Yardangs'. I realized that if one of the formations was carved into a statue it could be seen from the Nile. At that time Egypt was a fertile savannah. There was sufficient rain-fall. It was not the desert that it is today. The course of the Nile has changed since then. I made a drawing of what I wanted, and hired some workmen to help me with it. What was it to be, a lion's head, the head of a Queen, or King? Perhaps it would

15

be the head of a God or Goddess? I finally decided that it would be the head of a Goddess of Africa. At that time there were tribes from Africa that lived in the region, and they had been very kind to me. There were also Atlanteans there."

"Perhaps I was one of them…I don't remember. If there are heresies in this document that I am sending to you, so be it, my end is near. In this current incarnation, the face of the Goddess that I sculpted has been repaired many times, most recently by Kheffre many years ago. Before him Cheops tried to maintain and restore the statue."

"The Nile is no more near The Sphinx, and sand has buried the statues' secrets time and time again. Somewhere during the history of my work the body of a lion was added. It has been repaired many times and defaced as well, and yet I can still see the face of the Goddess-the main part of my work-again, I am old, and my imaginings may be the visions caused by blindness."

"When you sent me the message I became very excited. I remember the book! I remember seeing, and copying Vol II! I can almost remember what the pages looked like. There were drawings, designs, the text was barely understandable. In that incarnation I still remembered the ancient Atlantean language! I kept my copy of the book, a translation into a modern tongue. I don't think that I made more than one copy. I was never paid for my work, and there was some problem that I had with the

owner of the original book. I have no memory of what happened to the original. Pythagoras-there is a hidden chamber between the paws of the Lion's body that is now under my original head of the Goddess. I may have hidden the book there, or somewhere in the mile-long ramp that Hemiunu told me about when the Great Pyramid was being built. I don't remember. It saddens me to know that from one of my incarnations thousands of years ago to this one-my creation-the head of the Sphinx has been changed so much. I keep digressing."

"The problem here is that my memory wanders. I may have removed the book from the chamber between the paws at some time, fearing for its' safety under the mounting sands. I may have given it to my friend Hemiunu, to hide with his books inside the Great Pyramid of Giza. My memory grows dim. If you visit Egypt, I may be able to remember more, if I am still alive. Perhaps if Theoclea comes with you, she can help me to remember. I would very much like to meet her. I grow tired, and my Scribe is tired as well."

"I hope to see you one last time before…the three women come for me!"

The Scribe

"Vorios, as I said before, I've talked to Theoclea, Morain and Panelle about traveling to Egypt, and Theoclea was very excited, although Morain and Panelle are concerned for Theoclea's safety. Theoclea assured them that everything would be alright. I've also received messages from the Royal Court that reveals a great excitement about the visit of Theoclea, the children and the others."

" Once again, I'm going to suggest that we all make arrangements to leave for Egypt immediately. Morain and Panelle, of course, have resigned themselves to the fact that this is what Theoclea wants. We're taking the 'Star Children' along too...Alcena and Abderus. They may be very helpful to us Vorios."

Chapter Three... Pythagoras and Theoclea in the Rose Garden.

"Pythagoras, the prospect of all of us going on a trip to Egypt is exciting- for the children especially. I'd also like to see whether those bottles and the oils that I sent will help The Scribe's eyesight and memory. I've asked you to come here with any of the writings or the observations that you made during your youth and your studies in Egypt. I'd like to know more about what Egypt is like."

"I've been able to find some things, Theoclea, that I haven't looked at in many years. Before I became a priest, and a scientist, I created poetry in my youth, and it was written down by The Scribe. My teaching tradition is an oral one, and I have written nothing down myself. I leave that work to the scribes."

"Pythagoras, recite to me, the way that you did when I was your student. You always recited to me. I'd like to hear what you've found," Theoclea said.

"Well," Pythagoras replied, "I've found three pieces of poetry. I don't know whether they will give you an idea of what Egypt is like. Two of them may show you my thoughts at a certain time when I was a student in Egypt, Theoclea. The Scribe wrote them down for me. The last one was written when I was in Babylon, and it's a reflection of something that happened when I was in Egypt. I found a scribe in Babylon, who wrote it down for me."

"I want to hear the poetry," Theoclea replied. "Recite to me Pythagoras, I'd rather receive images and sounds from poetry than in almost any other way."

Here are the three poems that Pythagoras recited for Theoclea-

Summer Light,
The Tree,
and
The Pond

I sat on a bench at the
edge of a cliff,
overlooking a pond
that had been created by the overflowing of the Nile.
In the distance, I saw fishermen at the edge of the
pond.
Their nets revealed a meager catch
for the day. Slowly they went home.

Then, I saw something that I had never seen before.
To the left of me was a great tree
that grew on the edge of the cliff.
Suddenly, I saw bands of light
flowing inward towards the trunk
They started at the right
from the very edge of the smallest branches,
and flowed inward.
They reached the trunk
and then flowed outward
toward the very smallest branches to the left.

Each band could not have been more than six inches
in length.
There was a continuous movement of these bands
and then they vanished.

21

What was causing this?
I then noticed that a young boy
had thrown stones into the pond.
I watched him pass by,
and then disappear out of sight.

I then threw two stones into the pond,
and watched the waves that were created
when the stones hit the water.

Then, I witnessed
a solemn procession of Priests and Priestesses.
They could not see me
sitting on the bench near the tree.
I smelled their incense,
and heard their chanting.

I sensed that
It was possible that they were an illusion,
and that they could not see me,
the tree, or the bench.
None of them looked in my direction

They were looking at another tree,
another bench, in
another time.

My attention was brought back to the waves
in the pond

The motion of the waves
moving away from the two central points,
the interference caused by the waves,
all of this was being
reflected by the tree in its' entirety.
A seemingly chance coming together
of events of this particular day
at this place and time
had created a magical tree!

I have long felt that light and sound
are created by waves
that appear to us as something else.

On that particular day, at that particular moment,
something had been created.
I looked at the bands of light, and noticed
that they were all not the same size!
There was a minute difference in size and luminosity.
They were self-similar, and yet different.
I then decided to climb
down the cliff to the pond.

When I reached the pond,
I sat on a rock.
I looked toward my left and saw the dappled sunlight.

The sunlight reflected
a multitude of self-similar repeated patterns
of leaves, creating sparkling lights
that were hovering over the water.

Under the water, there seemed to be
A procession of green lights moving,
moving toward me,
yet never reaching me,
an army moving in, and then vanishing.

I was in Egypt for eleven years.
Every year on that day at that same time,
I returned to the same spot.

For eleven years I witnessed the
same illusions.
I smelled the same incense,
I heard the same chanting.
It was only on that day, at that time,
that I saw it all…

24

for I returned to the spot
at various other times during those years.

Finally, in my eleventh year,
it was all once again the same,
the fisherman with their meager catch,
the solemn procession that could not see me,
the bands of light moving across the tree.
The sparkling lights on the water
I didn't realize something-
that would be my last year in Egypt,
and I would never see any of it again.
I knew that for the rest of my life,
I would ponder these events,
especially on that day, at that time,
every year.

My Tent along the Nile

I once lived in a tent along the Nile
There were long afternoons when there were
breaks in my studies

I would lie on cushions and stare at the
light and the shadows
that played on the translucent ceiling.

Leaves, branches, and crawling insects
conspired to create a passing drama
(occasionally I heard the sound of a flute,
or a lone drummer).

There were nude women, statues,
skeletons, Chieftains and Chiefs
I saw the face of a scientist, heads with hats
of all kinds, puppets and Priests

I saw the great beasts
with their trunks raised high
Squirting water on the children
who lived in the East.

I saw the mouth of the Nile…
when the river gushes forth
A river that flows
from the South to the North.
No healing rainwater issued
from clouds in Egypt's skies,
yet the west wind blew the sand into my eyes,
and that is how many afternoons were spent
for all of this and more
I saw on the ceiling of my tent.

One fateful day, when I was pondering all of this,
The ceiling of my tent expanded into a huge white
dome.
I asked myself if this was a dream,
perhaps a vision while sleeping
near the Goddess-born foam

I heard instruments that made
a dub-dub sound
dub-dub, step-step
crunching all around,
in a myriad of beats
a cacophony of sound.

The music encircled me
going round and round!

Then images appeared,
on the ceiling of the dome.
And the sights and the sounds
were like reading an ancient tome
about strange buildings
all seen in black and white.
There were women in strange clothing,
Then the Goddess of the Night!

There were statues, and the spires
of a city by the sea.
There were fancy birds and dolphins' and things
yet to be!

There were endless repetitions in color
and black and white,
an infinite number of triangles
receding out of sight.

I pondered all of this and more,
when suddenly ferns started to appear on the floor.
And the dome, its sounds and images,
were not seen as before.

28

Surrounded by ferns, I saw a Goddess statue.
Her hair was red,
and she wore a black cape fringed in gold.
She wore a crown of golden crystals, pearls,
and gold lacing.
Her necklace and bodice were
also made of silver and gold crystals,
gold lacing, and pearls.

There was a crown of thorns hanging from a rock,
with crystal pendants hanging from the crown.

There were seashells and gemstones,
Mirrors and pinecones,
tumbled stones and Goddess statues,
rings and wristbands.
There was a small round mirror,
and Gods and Goddesses of yore.
There were bells, cats, angels,
necklaces, and more.
There were insects made of copper,
and Goddesses with wings,
a turtle made of Opaline, and many other things.
Then the clouds of sleep departed
and
I slowly made my way.

I opened my eyes gently
and beheld the light of day.
I gazed at the ceiling...
I had slept for awhile...
and once again...
I found myself...
in my tent along the Nile.

The Egyptian Woman...Eimon

In the prime of my youth
When my studies were rife
a strange dark-haired woman
appeared in my life

The daughter of a nobleman,
and I a Greek of little worth,
I was hired by her family
to teach the language of my birth.

Egypt was our meeting place
and when I saw her lovely face
my lonely heart beat no more
and nothing seemed as it was before
for time had stopped and from above

30

Eros' arrow had touched me-
I was entranced with love.

A glance from her as she walked in
Procession
was like Psyche's return
I was in her possession

Her name-Eimon
was whispered to me
and yet this was a love that was not to be.

Now I was studying to be a Priest
for it was an honor to say the least
that to study in Egypt, a land of Magic
was a joy for me, but the end was tragic

The Persian army, in an act not envisioned-
attacked Egypt and I was imprisoned.
My freedom was granted,
In an act of providence,
of the charges filed, there
was no evidence

I left Egypt and
saw Eimon no more

31

And slowly my life
returned as before.

In Babylon I now reside,
a man
whose studies allow no bride,
and yet, that face, the whisper,
that look,
of Eimon I dream
'tis like a book

Each page, each leaf
gives us love, pain, or grief.
I ponder the words,
I look for the meaning,
Yet thoughts of Eimon end my evening

I sometimes feel as I did before
I think of Egypt, Eimon, and more

Until I fall into sleep,
descending,
For the book, like love
Will find its' own ending

There were tears in Theocleas' eyes. She closed her eyes for about a minute. Then, she opened them, and smiled at Pythagoras.

"Pythagoras! You and I will return to that spot in the first poem. We'll go there on the same day, and be there at noon! Each of us will throw a stone into the Nile, and we'll see if the same thing happens again!"

"Perhaps also, there will be images that we shall see on the ceiling of our tent, and hear strange music as well."

She was silent for a few seconds, and then looked tenderly at him. "Perhaps we shall meet the woman who was the subject of your love poem. How will you feel about that?" Pythagoras looked at the ground and thought about what Theoclea had said.

"I was a youth when all of that happened. I'm not sure how I would feel."

"Pythagoras-there is a High Priestess in Egypt. I have seen her in a vision, and she has spoken to me. She is very wise, beautiful, and powerful, she is also a dancer, and her name is EIMON!"

Chapter Four... Theoclea questions Pythagoras

A few days later, Pythagoras met with Theoclea again in the Rose Garden.

"Pythagoras, I've had visions and dreams that have come to me at night, and at other times when I have inhaled the Dragon's breath in the Oracle's chamber, and prepared myself to go into trance and receive the pilgrim's questions for Apollo. The visions and dreams seem to involve our upcoming trip-I would like to have you and Vorios supply some information for me."

"About what?" Pythagoras replied.

"I've heard a name-Morvan, and I've seen someone talking and laughing. Who is he?"

Pythagoras was somewhat taken aback, but he had learned to expect the unexpected from Theoclea, her visions, and dreams.

"Morvan was in my class when I was first being trained to become a Priest in Egypt. He was a rival, and at times it was not a friendly rivalry. The games and puzzles presented to all of the initiates, especially in the realm of Egyptian Magic, always seemed to come down to the two us. He assumed the persona of a joker, a trickster. He was very glib, and always talking-an almost obsessive, compulsive talker. I had learned to shut out the clutter of his talk, and retain my focus when I was around him After a while, he lost interest in trying his tricks on me, knowing that they didn't work. He was always the one who had the most beautiful women around him, yet, I know for a fact that he was abusive to many of them. He was brilliant, though, and wrote extensively-although one of my teachers, 'The Scribe' would not write for him."

"Two more things, Pythagoras-did he write something about the Acausal Domain?"

"Where did you learn about that, Theoclea? You never cease to amaze me!"

"I…know of many things," Theoclea said coyly.

Pythagoras smiled, took her in his arms and kissed her passionately.

"I had no idea that my mention of the Acausal Domain would bring out such passion in you Pythagoras," she said.

36

He laughed. "Okay, once again," he shook his head and laughed. "Yes, Morvan wrote about the Acausal Domain. His primary thesis was on fluctuations in the Acausal Domain- and the realm of Ma'at"

Pythagoras studied her. "There's more, Theoclea."

"Yes, I know, Pythagoras. I'd like you and Vorios to get Morvan's papers and discuss them with me before we go to Egypt."

Theoclea hesitated for a moment, smiled, and said, "Pythagoras, what is a Hemp Bar?"

Pythagoras was stunned, and then stammered out an answer.

"It's...a place where men go to smoke a narcotic called hemp, and there are usually women there who sell their bodies-for sex, money and drugs."

"Thank you Pythagoras, you've enlightened me, as usual. Oh, one more thing, Eimon has a sister, a Jewish woman named Miriam. Her visage represents many paths that have come together to produce an enigmatic woman. I've seen her in my visions. Can you and Vorios find out as much about her as you can? Morain and Panelle can assist you."

Once again Pythagoras shook his head and laughed. "You used to have teams of spies that were employed by the Temple, and yet you claim that you've never needed them!"

"Theoclea, I know some things about Miriam. I remember that Miriam was there during the Greek lessons that I gave to Eimon. She was four or five years younger than Eimon, and an adopted sister. She was very attentive during the Greek lessons, and stood quietly by her sister's side- Eimon insisted that Miriam be there. Miriam was just a child, but she detested Morvan. I sensed that behind closed doors, she was the object of Morvan's mockery.

"Why, she was just a child?" Theoclea said.

"Well, Theoclea, Miriam was the child of a Jewish merchant and a Nubian woman- she was what we might call a child of mixed racial and ethnic heritage. I won't need the help of Vorios, Panelle, or Morain. I know the rest of the story. There was a Jewish merchant who came to the Royal Egyptian Court on a regular basis. He always had incense, herbs, potions and other things. He was especially revered by Eimon's father, because his medicines had saved the life of Eimon's mother. He always traveled with his wife, a woman from Nubia that he had met in his travels. Eventually they had a child- Miriam. For a few years the father, mother and child traveled together."

"Then, one year the merchant returned and told Eimon's father that his wife had died. He had Miriam with him. He himself was suffering from an illness that did not seem to be treatable by his potions. He asked Eimon's father, a wonderful, gracious, giving man, to take Miriam in for a year. If he did not return in one year, they were to assume that the illness had consumed him. Eimon's father told the Jewish merchant that he would treat Miriam as a sister to Eimon, and make sure that everyone was aware of the pledge that he made on that day."

"The Jewish merchant never returned, and Miriam became his adopted daughter after a year and a day, and was proclaimed to be a sister to Eimon. Eimon loved Miriam, and has always wanted Miriam to be at her side. Miriam has become a kind of a Protector/Guardian to Eimon-she has taken on this task of her own accord, and she is revered by most of the people in the family."

"They have survived the reign of Cambysus, the Persian, and it is a time of peace in Egypt. Cambysus was a ruthless man, killing many in his attack on Egypt. After the attack was successful and the reign of the Pharoahs was ended, Cambysus ordered 50,000 men into the desert to attack Nubia and seize the gold mines."

"The 50,000 men were never seen again. Cambysus was called back to answer to the rulers of Persia, and they were harsh with him, and sent an entirely different

Persian man rule to Egypt. He is a great admirer of Egyptian culture, and is betrothed to Eimon."

"Thank you Pythagoras, that is all of the information that I need about Miriam and Eimon. Oh yes, I would like you to discuss the science and magic of numbers that the Egyptians believe in with Vorios-I think that if both of you possess that knowledge it may be of benefit to us. There may be other questions that I shall have." She smiled and said, "and I'll take note that the mention of the Acausal Domain arouses a passion in you."

Chapter Five... Egyptian Numbers

They had decided to meet at one of the outdoor altars, and there was a stairway that went up the mountainside that was used to get to the altar. Vorios reached the end of the stairs, opened the gate and saw that Pythagoras was already there. The large crystal was on the altar, and Pythagoras was studying it. He put it down gently when he saw Vorios. Three crows then landed on the crystal and watched them.

"Pythagoras, you're my teacher today. I want to know some of the secrets of the Egyptians. Let's start with their number system"

"Ah, Vorios, you've started with the hardest part, you see in Egypt, all is one, the religion, the numbers, the calendars, and especially the buildings, all is connected. The buildings are their books. They have very few books as we know of them. Their numbers, calendars, weights and measures, and everything else is presented not only in the picture language on the walls, but the proportions contained in the architecture of the buildings. It all speaks volumes about the Egyptians. The actually use three calendars!"

"How was it that all of this came into being, almost 4000 years ago? Many believe that there was no development that can be seen in the growth of these ideas... many believe that they are the legacy of Atlantis. I'll get back to that sometime later. Let me tell you about the numbers."

"The Egyptians have developed something I call 'Sacred Science'. They are aware of a subtler metaphysical reality-their hieroglyphics, or picture words say something to both the 'ordinary people', and the 'initiates'. The ordinary common people use a kind of a 'demotic' language, but they have an understanding of the thinking behind the picture-language."

"We have degenerated into what we have in Greece, through 'reason'. Our language stops us from thinking in other ways. The Temple of Luxor, in Egypt, for instance tells the story of the Cosmos and man's place in it. Each room speaks of different harmonic relationships and concepts of proportion. The story is not in a book, but the building, the architecture is a book in itself."

"The numbers-'the many are derived from the one' as the Egyptians say. I wish that we had, in Greece, a feeling of oneness with the Cosmos. The Cult of Osiris speaks of reincarnation and renewal. Art, Science, Myth, all represent an organic unity. Think of the pyramids-they embody in their dimensions a great deal of astronomical, and mathematical information. Even geographic and what I like to call 'geodesic' information is contained in those structures."

"I was taught the importance of harmony and proportion. I was taught about irrational numbers, and higher concepts like PI and PHI...the 'Golden Section'. This may all sound new to you, Vorios, but their picture symbols contain a hierarchy of meanings from the most literal to the abstract."

"Take the symbol for the EYE, for instance. In the most obvious interpretation, it is the eye, it is vision, perhaps the all-seeing eye of a God or Goddess. But they usually draw the eye in exact proportion, in a stylized way, and if you looked at each part of the drawing you would see an exact representation of their fractional system of measurement-the pupil being perhaps ¼, the left part of the eye being $1/16$, the right part being ½...and so on until you will see that all of the fractions from $1/64^{th}$ to ½ are exactly represented in all of the parts of a stylized 'eye'."

"My God!" said Vorios- "I had no idea of this!"

"There's more, Vorios, and most of it known only to the Initiates. I was very fortunate, Vorios, as a foreigner, to have been considered to be one of them. It took some time for me to gain their trust."

"The number one, represents the absolute, unity, that creates the other numbers from itself. One becomes two by the process of something called 'Primordial Scission'."

"Two is a very divisive number, it is the fall into chaos, the call to polarity, polarization, Seth and Horus-a kind of primordial tension."

"Three may be thought of as being reconciliation, relationship between opposing forces, with a third force reconciling them. Think of the artist, who may have inspiration, and skill, but a third thing, a passion for the art is needed to bring the three together. I'm not sure that that is best analogy, but it will have to do."

"The number four introduces us to a new concept-the material world-for in the end we have the art work, the actual painting."

"Five and Six-Five is the number of 'love' or life, the union that creates the event. The four terms that I used before are insufficient to create the event. I'm talking here about a consistent structure that is the underpinning of our reality, for without five, the creative union, the event doesn't take place."

"Six-The five things that I've described take place somewhere, and that place is Space and Time. Without Six, we have no reference as to where, and when-we have no comparisons. We can't see, or visualize any of this without knowing the framework."

"Seven represents 'growth' the act of 'becoming'. Growth is hard for us to grasp, but in most of our experience, change and growth occur."

"The growth may be so slow that we cannot see it, or measure it, but we see our own growth. We are born-we live-and we die. The growth is not continuous, sometimes it seems to stop, and then as if from a preconceived principle it starts again."

"Eight-is the eighth sign of the Zodiac-'Scorpio'. It is Thoth-our Hermes-'The Master of the city of Eight', who gives us language, knowledge, magic and the mysteries"

"The numbers nine, ten, eleven and twelve defy our language capabilities. They exist in the higher realm of the complex world of 'possibilities'. Think of the thirty pieces in the KeyRose Box, often called 'The box of possibilities', and you can begin to realize that perhaps these concepts can be made relevant only through images."

Vorios stood there in complete silence for a few minutes, trying to comprehend all that Pythagoras had said.

"You have truly amazed me, my friend. I've always heard that you were the finest teacher that anyone could ever have. The reputation that follows you, the school curriculum that you have created-it's all an oral tradition, and to hear all of this from you, with such clarity and passion is something that I shall never forget."

"We have had so many wonderful discussions,"… Vorios was searching for the words…"and yet, I shall never forget this one!"

"Perhaps I should ponder all that you have said, and wait for our arrival in Egypt before I even ask you to explain their magic."

Pythagoras smiled, and said "Vorios, for once, I have left you speechless, my brother." Pythagoras smiled… and they embraced each other as brothers will, a scientist, and a magician.

Chapter Six...Miriam and Eimon

Miriam and Eimon were walking through an arbor that had been created as an adjunct to the Temple of Luxor. They had taken a much needed break from the Royal Court activities to travel to Thebes with a small entourage of other women and men from the Court. They walked around the temple admiring the hieroglyphics and the architecture of the old temple. Then they sat down for a chat. Eimon was wearing her characteristic red, black and gold. She varied her dress with the occasion, wearing the ceremonial red tiara, and black robe with gold lacing and cords for formal occasions-today she wore a gold tunic, black cord, and a red headband for informal walks and daily activities. She wore a solid gold talisman, or amulet with the form of a scarab engraved on it. The beaded necklace that held it around her neck was made of solid gold beads as well.

She had lately taken to having her hair dyed red, but the fashion had not caught on with the other Egyptian women. Miriam was walking with the ever-present spear in her left hand. The spear was sharp, and had a gold, black and white ribbon on the top of it. Her black curly hair had strands of gold at the top and they were waving in the breeze. She always wore make-up, not quite as ornate as the makeup of Egyptian men and women, but just enough. She wore large gold earrings with black tassels hanging down from them, as well as an ornate collar with a purple neckband, and red, blue and gold striping that covered her shoulders.

Gold tassels hung from the shoulders, and around her neck was a beaded solid gold necklace that had been given to her by Eimon on one of her birthdays.

There was also a beaded necklace that held a large gold bag that hung from the end of it. Her top was simple- it was red with blue bands at the edges. The top concealed a corded belt that held yet another large gold bag. Her skirt was black and white and reflected the pattern of zebra stripes that she was so fond of.

She called the way that she was dressed that day 'The Nubian Warrior's Costume'. It reminded her of her self-assumed role as the protector of her sister-the High Priestess Eimon.

48

They were standing in front of a low table that had various gold black and red bottles of various sizes. Miriam stared at the hieroglyphics, and a picture of a serpent caught her attention. She raised her spear and pointed to it.

"If you know the magical spell you can make the serpent appear just by pointing at it. The magicians of the past knew how to do it. I'm not sure what the Egyptian magicians of today can do. I am certainly not impressed with Morvan!" Miriam said.

Eimon decided to change the subject. "Let's not to talk about that man. I get the chills when I'm around him."

There was a pause in the conversation. They were in a large room that had hieroglyphics on all the walls, as well as scenes on the ceiling.

"Miriam, where do you go on Saturdays, you've always been so secretive about that?"

"I go to a place where I can commune with my ancestors, and others of like mind. We talk about the past, present and future."

In a sense, Miriam was raised by all of the members of the Royal Court, and her adopted father had insisted that she be raised alongside Eimon. Yet, she was different from Eimon. She took to mathematics in a way

49

that surprised everyone. She had adopted Ma'at as her patron Goddess, at the same time observing Judaism and its' ways and traditions privately.

"Miriam, I am to be married soon to the Persian man who is taking Cambysus' place. He's so different from Cambysus…he's very sympathetic to Egyptian ways-I've been with him a few times, and I think that he'll make a fine husband. What do you think, Miriam?"

"He's undoubtedly a fine man, you are very fortunate, Eimon," Miriam said, as she sighed and looked down at the ground.

"Miriam-is there a man that you see on Saturdays?" Eimon asked.

"No, Eimon, although I think that meeting a foreigner, perhaps a Greek man would feel right to me, although I think that it would be against Jewish Law to do that. You know that the Jewish Priests, or Rabbis are not like Egyptian Priests. They are teachers and scribes. They engage in debates about Jewish Law. I take my day of meditation from sundown on Friday to sundown on Saturday. I know the holy books of Judaism, especially the Torah and I can read in Hebrew. My father taught me this. I know a lot about Moses, as well," Miriam said.

Miriam was uncomfortable about talking about her Saturdays, and Eimon sensed this. How could Miriam ever tell anyone about the medallion that her father had given her? She had learned to use it, and had a vague idea of who was depicted on the face side. Her merchant father had told her that it was the rarest treasure in the world, and she was to guard it with her life. She was to reveal its' existence to only one person. She kept it with her at all times in one of the gold bags.

"Okay, Miriam, I'll respect your privacy. I just wish that there was a Jewish man around here for you. You are also part Nubian, and the Nubians are all rich with the gold mines being down there. Perhaps a rich Nubian..."

She paused and sensed that it would be better to change the subject.

"Everyone is excited about the visit of Theoclea, the Delphic Oracle, Pythagoras, the teacher, and their entourage. Do you remember Pythagoras? He was the handsome student who taught us Greek."

"That was many years ago," said Miriam, "but I remember. He also talked about Mathematics, and Geometry that he had learned in our country. I liked that part of his teachings. I'm afraid that I've forgotten all of the Greek phrases that he taught us."

"He also taught for a year and a day at the Temple of Delphi, and was the Priest at the Portal of Theoclea's Initiation. I wonder what he taught her?" Eimon said.

Miriam raised her eyes in disbelief at her sister's naivete.

She smiled, and then said "I'm sure that he taught her a lot." They have two children, and if you look at the calendar, they must have been conceived when..." She said no more, wishing to change the subject.

"I'm more interested in Theoclea," Miriam said. "Have you read her book, 'Whispers'?"

"Of course," said Eimon, "although I must admit that I had parts of it read to me. They say that when she gave the speech at Eleusis a Phoenix appeared in the sky. She spoke as the cloud dissipated, and then two lightning flashes crossed from two different directions underneath the cloud. Do you know that the lightning flashes and the cloud are her personal symbol? What a way to end a speech...I wonder how the magic was done?"

"I'm interested in the medallion-the Rose Medallion that she sometimes wears," said Miriam. "She used it in her Eleusis speech. She stared at the face side of the medallion for a minute. You know that the face side shows the image of the goddess Inanna-the ancient Sumerian Goddess whose symbol was The Rose. Anyway, she stared at it, and then turned it over and said very dramatically "The Medallion Speaks!" I would have liked to have been there when she used the medallion. Parts of the speech were taken from her book. It is said that part of her power is in her choice of words."

"I can't wait to meet her," Eimon said. "I've heard that she can walk into a room and in one sentence she can capture everyone's attention."

"I'm curious to see how her extraordinary gifts come into play in her everyday conversations and interactions with people. It is hard to imagine that she sees that past present and future in her visions. She hears the whispers…she sees…she is the eyes and ears of our time-not only for Greece, but for Egypt as well I suspect. 'I hear, I see…I speak not only to those who are in front of me, but to those in the future time of renewal.'-that's a quote from her book, Eimon"

Chapter Seven...The children prepare for the trip

Pythogaras walked over to the children's quarters. Alcena, and Abderus still lived with the rest of the orphans, but in separate quarters, with a guard always outside their room. The fact that they were the children of Pythagoras and Theoclea was now well known at the Temple, and everyone agreed that a certain amount of protection was needed for them. Their lives went on, they continued to attend the classes, and the other orphans were instructed to be protective of them, which was no problem-they were well loved and respected by their peers.

Pythagoras saw Abderus leaving his quarters. Abderus walked over to the guard that was in front of Alcena's room and whispered something. The guard opened the door, then closed it, and whispered something to him. Abderus smiled and nodded, then turned, and saw Pythagoras coming down the hallway.

"Abderus, just the one that I wanted to speak to. Come, my boy, let's go outside where we won't be disturbed." They walked around a corner and found a spot in a garden with secluded benches. Abderus noticed that Pythagoras had two packages in his arms. Pythagoras spotted a bench and said, "Sit down, my boy, we have a lot to talk about, is your sister, Alcena around?"

"No, Pythagoras, I checked with the guard, and she's still sleeping."

"That's okay, you can relate to her the substance of our conversation, and give her the package." Pythagoras placed two packages on the bench beside them. He leaned closer to Abderus and said,

"While we're in Egypt, there's a secret mission that will occur, and Vorios and I have decided to include both of you in the mission!"

"A Secret Mission!" Abderus said. Pythagoras looked around to see if anyone was listening, and then continued.

"I can't tell you the details, yet, but we shall be searching for something. You don't know this, and don't tell anyone of this but your sister...Vorios, the chief magician at the Temple has given me...The Medallion of Hermeticus!"

"No!" said Abderus.

"Yes, and certain truths have been revealed to me. I've seen the writings of the future, and people who look for clues and solve mysteries are called 'detectives' in the future!"

"Detectives!" said Abderus.

"Yes, and I see something wonderful in you- the ability to express yourself in words...an ability way beyond your years!

"Well," Abderus said, modestly," I wouldn't hardly put it that way."

Pythagoras looked around once again to see if anyone was listening, and then returned to Abderus.

"You needn't be modest, my boy. I've heard your poetry. I especially like the 'Dark Night of the Soul' poem. Your sister, Alcena has a keen mind and a gift for singing, and writing her own songs. She has also had visions, like your mother, Theoclea. These are gifts that are only given to a special few by the Gods, and the Goddesses. On this mission, you may even witness some of Vorios' magic, and perhaps my own magic"

"Magic!" Abderus said.

"Yes," Pythagoras said, "...and you might meet 'The Spirits of Eternal Vigilance'!"

"The Spirits of Eternal Vigilance?" Abderus said, his eyes growing wider as Pythagoras spoke.

Pythagorus looked around to see if anyone else was listening.

"Beware...of the Muhajihadeem!"

"The Muhajihadeem?" Abderus said.

"You and your sister both have keen minds, and are adventurous. It makes sense, given that Theoclea and I are your parents. These qualities may be helpful in solving some Mysteries!"

"Mysteries!" Abderus said.

"Now, here are my instructions to you, for now. In Egypt, if you ever see a crystal in the shape of an Pentagon, you are to immediately look to your left or right, and if see a crystal in the shape of a Tetrahedron about ten feet away, then there will undoubtedly be a crystal about fifteen to twenty feet in front of you, in the shape of an Obelisk- forming a triangle of crystals. You are not to step inside that triangle, it is a trap! Is that clear?"

"Yes, Pythagoras-A Triangle Crystal Trap!" Abderus said.

"Now if the Crystals are a Five-pointed star, a Sphere and an Egg, then you are standing in a triangle of healing, safety and protection, and that's okay, got it?"

"Yes," said Abderus.

"Now, there may be more that I will have to tell you in Egypt. Take these packages and give one to your sister. Do you swear on the memory of one the oldest Oracles, Phoebe, not to mention this to anyone except your sister?"

"I swear!" said Abderus.

"You sister must swear the same oath, can I trust you with that responsibility?"

Yes, Pythagoras,"said Abderus.

"One more thing, Pythagoras, what was that word that you used from the future, to describe people who solve mysteries and look for clues?"

"Detectives!" said Pythagoras.

"Okay, Abderus, I trust that you will continue to protect your sister. I've noticed this quality in you and it is a most admirable trait!"

"Hardly a day goes by when I don't have to protect her from something! By the way, Pythagoras, does our mother, Theoclea know of this?"

Pyhagoras sighed, "Theoclea seems to know of everything, even those things that I don't tell her about. Believe me, she knows!"

Pythagoras then took his leave of Abderus, and Abderus walked back to his quarters with both packages.

He turned around and smiled as Abderus left. His years of teaching young people were having an effect-on his own son and daughter!

Abderus saw Alcena emerging from her room and gave her one of the packages. He looked around, saw the guard, and said, "follow me." He led her around the corner to the garden and the bench. He related his conversation with Pythagoras. She was indignant.

"Why was I not included in this conversation?" she asked.

"Because...you were asleep!" Abderus said.

"True," she nodded.

"Detectives- Vorios-Pythagoras- Magic," she said.

"So, we're being asked to participate in a Secret Mission. We are to be like 'detectives', looking for clues. We might meet 'The Spirits of Eternal Vigilance'-see 'Muhajihadeem'- and look for 'Crystal Triangle Traps'.

"She grabbed Abderus and and hugged him. "Don't you see-this is a mystery, and mystery surrounds me-mystery finds me!"

They then opened the packages-The packages contained crystal lanterns, magnifying glasses, small whisk brooms, hammers and chisels of different sizes, and much more.

They looked at each other with wide eyes, and then Alcena said "What are Muhajihadeem?"

Abderus shrugged, and said "I don't know, he didn't hardly tell me, but don't worry, I'll protect you! Now there is an oath that you must swear..."

Chapter Eight... The entrance of Theoclea and the others into the Royal Court.

A few days later the boats were ready, and Theoclea and her entourage sailed the Mediterranean. The trip was uneventful, and eventually they arrived in Egypt. They immediately traveled to Cairo over land, while tents were set up for them on the Giza plateau. The Persians had made Cairo, near Giza their headquarters, and it had become the new Capital City of Egypt. Theoclea and the others had their belongings unloaded, and the campsite was prepared. The children found many things to occupy their time, and children from the Royal Court had been sent to play with them. Two days later Theoclea, Pythagoras, and others were presented formally to the Royal Court.

Theoclea and her entourage waited in an anteroom, waiting to be introduced to their Egyptian hosts. In the room next door, called the Grand Court, everything was being made ready for the entrance of Theoclea, Pythagoras, and the others.

In the Court, Morvan, the Chief Magician of the Royal Court was talking to a group of men.

"You do know that the children are the illegitimate children of Pythagoras and Theoclea, am I right, gentlemen?"

"Of course we do," one of the men replied. "Morvan, where were you when the news of Pythagoras and Theoclea was circulated-it's common knowledge. We've all been instructed to look out for the welfare of the children. They are to meet all of our children, and your children as well, Morvan-at least the ones that you've told us about." The men all laughed.

In the next room, Theoclea sat in a corner, her eyes closed, deep in concentration. She heard whispers- "Well, gentlemen there's a joke that has been circulating-it goes like this-Theoclea, the Oracle, Cambyses, the Persian, and the Architect of the Great Giza Pyramid, Hemiunu meet in a hemp bar...and-

Theoclea was abruptly interrupted out of her daydream and saw three amorphous light shapes flittering about the ceiling of the room. They whispered to her, and she smiled, thankfully. Pythagoras, Vorios, Morain and Panelle had been whispering while Theoclea appeared to be meditating. No one seemed to be aware of the light-shapes on the ceiling.

Suddenly, the doors flung wide open, and a Herald announced:

"Theoclea, the Oracle of the Temple of Delphi, accompanied by Pythagoras, Priest and Master of Sacred Geometry, and their entourage!"

Pythagoras took Theoclea's hand and they walked into the room.

There was a receiving line, and the first one in line was Morvan, the Magician-The Herald announced him-"Morvan, the Chief Magician of the Egyptian Royal Court", and a hush fell over the room.

Theoclea walked toward him a few steps, and said:

"I am pleased to meet you. You must agree, Morvan, that it is very unlikely that you would ever find me in a hemp bar, certainly not with Cambysus- he was a tyrant! But I would like to have met Hemiunu, the architect of the Great Pyramid, perhaps in a vision. Seeing me in a hemp bar would be like a strange fluctuation in the acausal realm. I have read your papers and look forward to discussing them with you, and of course, our children (she motioned to Pythagoras) will be looking forward to playing with your children, all of your children!" She smiled a knowing smile, and smiled at all of the men around Morvan. There was a hush, and everyone had heard the exchange. They all knew of Morvan's tasteless joke.

She had broken the ice, and had won almost everyone over with just a few sentences. She bowed her head toward Morvan and the others, and continued down the line. Pythagoras briefly faced Morvan, He nodded and said:

"Morvan, my old rival."

Morvan said, "Pythagoras, we shall have to play a game of Gemaia."

"What, you would let me beat you again?" Pythagoras smiled and moved on.

The men around Morvan were laughing quietly at these exchanges. Morvan smiled, then turned and glared at them.

Having heard her exchange with Morvan, everyone wanted to meet Theoclea. Pythagoras, and of course, Morain, Panelle, and Vorios, were in a very delicate situation of being gracious, and vigilant at the same time. The room had columns about four feet high, and they all had large oil lamps that provided the light. The

Egyptian writing was on all of the walls. Pythagoras was momentarily diverted from his thoughts. The meaning of the picture writing all started to come back to him. The light from the oil lamps was warm and comforting, yet full of forebodings. For some reason, the crystal lanterns had been abandoned in Egypt. They had simply stopped working, one by one.

Finally, Theoclea stood in front of Miriam. Again a hush fell over the room.

"Miriam, the beloved adopted sister of Eimon, and her Protector" was announced by the Herald. Miriam stared at Theoclea, she was not prepared for a woman who wore no makeup and had a child-like look to her. Yet, Miriam knew that Theoclea was in her mid-forties, and dressed in the most formal red, gold and black colors of her standing. She said to Theoclea,

"It is the fulfillment of a dream-I have always wanted to meet you-what an honor for me," she said. She was dressed in her 'protectors' costume, as she called it, the 'costume of a 'Nubian Warrior'. Her spear was sharp. She was an adopted daughter, the child of a Jewish merchant and a Nubian woman.

Theoclea looked at Miriam and there were tears in her eyes. She walked forward and embraced Miriam. She looked at Miriam with more tears, and said "Eimon's sister, and my sister as well." She then embraced Miriam again and whispered to her-"Miriam, we shall talk soon-about your medallion." Tears welled up in Miriam's eyes as well.

'*She knows, SHE KNOWS*', Miriam thought. Theoclea placed both hands on either side of Miriam's face and nodded. "It is both a curse and a blessing, I *see* and I *know*, she whispered." She then blinked the tears away and smiled at Miriam. "I have a gift for you," Theoclea said. Panelle passed the gift to Theoclea. She gave Miriam a KeyRose box set that had been especially designed for the occasion. It was in a plain box with a strange stone medallion on the top. Miriam looked at it and said, "Thank you, Theoclea." She was still crying. Everyone in the court was impressed. They wondered what had been said to Miriam-she was a beloved daughter to everyone.

Miriam composed herself, took Theoclea's hand and they walked over to Eimon.

"Oracle-Theoclea, may I introduce to you my sister, Eimon."

It was Theoclea's turn to be shocked, taken completely aback. Eimon, with her red hair, wearing the colors- the red, black and gold of Axcelotl, the last Queen of Atlantis- looked like a young Axcelotl. Theoclea stood before her, and said, "I had a speech prepared...

68

but you look so much like someone that I...she looked all about-there was a hush, and everyone was listening. "You look so much like-a great woman that I...saw in a vision"...she moved forward-she had once again broken down into tears and embraced Eimon. "You look so much like her! She was my Ancient Mother, and I was the child."

Once more, everyone in the room, except for Morvan, the Magician, was deeply affected by the few words that Theoclea said. Morain held the gift for Eimon, and handed it to Theoclea, along with a handkerchief to dry her tears. "This KeyRose box was specially designed by a man named 'The Merchant' for this occasion," Theoclea said. The box was a black lacquer box, with a silver medallion on the top, encrusted with jewels. Eimon received the gift, rushed forward and embraced Theoclea. Eimon said,

"I speak for everyone...your words have touched us...we all know of your greatness...and we look forward to the message that you will bring us, when you speak between the paws of the statue-The Sphinx. Theoclea, that was my speech, but I can remember no more of it-I am so deeply touched." She embraced Theoclea and held Theoclea's tear-stained face in both hands. "My new sister, Theoclea, will you accept me as that?" Theoclea was once again given the handkerchief by Morain. She wiped her tears, and said "of course I accept you as my sister."

Eimon took Theoclea's hand and escorted her to a third woman. The third woman, of course would have been the counselor, an Empath like Morain. "This is Priori, my Counselor. Theoclea looked at the woman, and knew that she was the woman in the vision that she had the night before. She walked forward and embraced Priori. She whispered in her ear. *"In the end, do not follow him. You will know when not to follow him. You are a free woman and you have your own free will!"*

Priori was stunned, she had not expected a prophecy from this woman. She embraced Theoclea and whispered "You know, you know of my troubles." Theoclea, whispered *"Yes, I See, and I Know-and you will know what to do when the time comes. I know this to be true. You are a brave woman"* Panelle handed Theoclea a gift, it was the same gift that had been given to Miriam, the plain box, with the strange stone on the top. "Thank you Theoclea-Oracle of Delphi, Priori said. I know of these boxes of prophecy, I will try to use it wisely."

Theoclea turned and faced everyone in the room, and said,

"I am deeply touched by your hospitality. I look forward to speaking to all of you when I deliver my speech between the paws of your greatest statue...the most well-known statue in the world, The Sphinx. I bring you a message from the Greek people, for I am their eyes and ears-but I am your eyes and ears as well. I See, I know, and I hear the whispers. We are all one. I speak to those of you, in the past, present, and future. You shall all see, and hear as well." She paused, and looked at everyone in the room. "Thank you for inviting me. I hope...that my words...and my visions will inspire you."

"I have been on a path that started with finding a Pan statue, and a Treasure chest with a Red Key on it, when I was playing with my friends Anka and Troyana, when we were children, and I had my first vision, the falling of a tree, and more. I have never strayed from that path, and finally, that path has led me here. I am Theoclea, the Pythian Priestess, the Oracle of the great Temple of Delphi, I am the Dragon Priestess of the Earth, the Pythia, the Pythoness. I am a Priestess of Apollo and Dionysus." She then held up the bag that she had brought with her. "I wear the Red Key of Orpheus,"- she put it around her neck. She reached into the bag and took out the Rose Medallion, held it up, and said for all to hear. "I am a Priestess of Inanna,

71

one of the oldest of the Goddesses as well-her symbol was The Rose. Thank you, one and all. Blessed Be." She bowed to everyone Morain handed her the tear-stained handkerchief and there were hugs and 'Blessed Be's' exchanged all around the room. Everyone was deeply impressed, and in tears-except for one, who stood in the corner, his arms folded, and watched the scene. The oil lamps flickered for a moment, but remained strong.

Chapter Nine...They visit the Scene of the Poem, and meet 'The Scribe'

The next day was to be a fateful day for Theoclea. Pythagoras had promised to take her to see 'The Scribe' in the afternoon. In the morning, they were to go to the spot that Pythagoras described in the poem, 'Summer light, the tree, and the Pond.' They had planned this before the trip-they looked at the calendar, and knew that this day was the day when he always saw the illusion of the patterns on the tree, and the passing ghostly procession.

They had a light breakfast, and then proceeded to the spot, for it was within walking distance of their tent. They found the bench at the edge of the cliff, overlooking the pond, and they saw the fishermen. They watched the great tree that grew at the edge of the cliff. As they sat there, they each took a stone, and threw it into the pond. Then, moments later they saw the bands of light flowing inward from the right toward the trunk, starting from the edge of the smallest branches and flowing inward. When they reached the trunk, the bands flowed outward toward the very smallest branches on the left.

Then, they witnessed the solemn procession of Priests and Priestesses. They smelled the incense, and heard the chanting. One of the priestesses turned and smiled-she *saw* Theoclea.

"That has never happened before!" Pythagoras said. The procession went on. Theoclea smiled at the woman-They saw each other, then Theoclea closed her eyes. After about a few minutes of meditating, Theoclea said-"Let's walk down to the pond-I want to do everything that you did in the poem."

They climbed down the cliff to the pond, sat on the rock and watched the dappled sunlight that reflected the patterns of the leaves, and the sparkling lights that hovered over the water. They saw the procession of green lights under the water, moving toward them, but never reaching them.

Pythagoras said, "no one in that procession ever looked at me during the eleven years that I came to this spot on this day every year. Yet today, being here with you-one of the women smiled and looked at you, Theoclea. What happened?" Theoclea smiled at Pythagoras and took his hand.

"She was Hatshepsut, the only woman in Egypt's history to become a Pharoah, over nine hundred years ago. I have seen her before in my visions," Theoclea said. They both sat on the rock and looked over at the fishermen. Instead of a meager catch, their nets were full-it was the best catch that they had in hundreds of years. Pythagoras stared at them and the full catch in their nets. He then turned to Theoclea. She was smiling, as she gazed at the fisherman.

That afternoon, they went to see 'The Scribe'. He lived in a simple white tent, again, within walking distance of the pyramids and the Sphinx. They entered the tent, and Pythagoras immediately had the feeling that he had been there before-there was something familiar about it. When he was a student The Scribe lived in Thebes, and his chambers were in the Temple of Luxor-the school was in Thebes as well.

In the middle of the tent, there was a circular table with some food spread out on it, and sitting at the side of the table was The Scribe. Pythagoras said, "Are we interrupting something, my old teacher?" The man laughed and clapped his hands joyfully.

"Pythagoras-I would recognize that voice any time! Pythagoras, come here!" Pythagoras quickly walked over to the old man and put his arms around him. There were tears in the old man's eyes.

"I cannot see you, I am blind-but that voice-how I have longed to hear it again. Pythagoras, you were my finest student. I'm always hearing great things about you." They embraced once again.

Then, The Scribe said, "Is she here?" Did you bring her?"-Is Theoclea here?"

"Yes," Pythagoras said, and he went back to the doorway, and took Theoclea's hand. Pythagoras placed Theoclea's hand in one of The Scribe's hands.

"What a surprise and an honor, I am finally meeting Pythagoras' teacher-his mentor. He has always talked about you in the most glowing terms-Please accept my humble thanks for teaching the man who became my teacher," Theoclea said.

The Scribe was in tears.

"I am the one to be humble on this occasion. I am meeting the great Theoclea-your words have been read to me, and now, to actually hear you speak-I know your words-they are engraved on my memory."

"*I see, I hear-I am the eyes and ears not only of Greece, but of the whole world. It is both a blessing and a curse.*" You

76

see, I have read your words. Please join me, both of you, in a simple repast. I have had food brought in for this occasion."

They sat down and The Scribe continued. "You are both a Priestess of Apollo, and Dionysus, Theoclea, am I right?"

"Yes, and I also follow the Goddess Inanna to achieve balance," Theoclea replied.

"A wise choice, my dear. As a Priestess of Dionysus, I must say that I have no wine to serve you-Those jars over there are all filled with water." Theoclea looked over at the jars, and said,

"I think that you will find that the last jar contains wine, and if it does, I would certainly like to share a glass with both of you. Pythagoras, would you check that last jar?" Theoclea said.

Pythagoras frowned, stood up and walked over to the jars. They were all sealed with corks. He pulled the cork out of the last jar and smelled the liquid, he then dipped a finger into it and exclaimed-

"It is filled with wine...How..." He looked over at Theoclea, and she smiled, and said "Then, let's all have a glass-there is much that we have to talk about!"

The Scribe said, "Pythagoras, don't ever leave this woman's side. She's a treasure! She must have known that I filled that last jar some time ago. She must have seen it in a vision. Don't ever let this woman go! Come, let's have a glass-there are three glasses on the table. Pythagoras fill them up!"

They all laughed, but Pythagoras was still a little perplexed, as he brought the jar over, and filled the glasses.

"Theoclea, I've been drinking that liquid that you sent to me every day, and using the oils on my eyes, but I haven't noticed any difference in my memory or any improvement in my eyesight."

"Perhaps there are other things that we can try," Theoclea replied.

They talked about many things, and agreed to meet again the following afternoon. Later, they said their goodbyes, and Pythagoras and Theoclea left. As they were walking back, Theoclea stopped, and faced Pythagoras.

"He's blind, and I know that you were disappointed about how little he remembers. I know that you were counting on his memories about the book." Pythagoras nodded. "Yes, I thought that he would remember more. He was still thinking about the wine in the jar.

Theoclea hesitated and then said, "You know that I am a healer. I received the gift of healing from the

Dancer, The Lady in White, on the cliff overlooking the doomed capital city of Atlantis."

"Yes," Pythagoras said. "You told me that you were able to take a thorn out of your cat's paw and the bleeding stopped-the wound healed immediately. I remember that you finally told me that."

"There's more, Pythagoras, much more. The power has grown in the months that you've been away. I believe that I can restore The Scribe's eyesight, and restore his memory-but I fear that it will only last a few days, maybe a week or more at the most. I had hoped that the liquid and the oils that I sent would work. I see now that they haven't worked. If I can restore his eyesight and memory, he will have to pretend that he is blind for the time that my healing works. It would be dangerous for people to know that I can do this."

They walked back to their tent in silence. Pythagoras was deep in thought. When they reached the tent, Pythagoras turned to her and said, "He would have to agree to try this. He has his own free will. I know him, but if it were possible-if you said that you could do it, it would be an immense help to us in completing our search. He would have to want to try it, knowing that it would not last. How do you know that you can do this, Theoclea?"

"Morain's eyesight has been getting worse over the years. This year, it started to deteriorate rapidly. She suffered a head injury one day-she fell when she was climbing the stairs to the upper Rose Garden. When Panelle found her, she was completely unconscious, and Panelle summoned me immediately. You know that there is a mental bond between the three of us. Morain's head was injured and she was bleeding profusely. She had minor bruises here and there as well. I placed my hands on her head, shared my aura with hers for a few minutes. When she became conscious she felt her head-the blood was gone and the wound had healed."

"Morain looked around and exclaimed 'I can see the railing, before I couldn't see it, I knew that my eyesight was failing, but didn't want to discuss it with anyone. But now,' she quickly looked around, and said, 'now I can see everything!' She closed her eyes for about thirty seconds, and when she opened them, she said, 'I also seem also to be able to remember things that I had forgotten-you've improved my memory as well!' I checked her for the bruises, and they were gone as well. I needed to do this sharing of the aura only once more several months later. Morain is not what we consider to be old yet, and so the healing has lasted. I cannot say for certain how long the healing would last for The Scribe-he is old, and has had the blindness and the memory loss for some time now."

Pythagoras reached out to Theoclea and held her in his arms.

They kissed, and held the passionate warm embrace. Then he held her shoulders at arms length and looked into her eyes.

"You surprise me and enchant me-you are a mystery-The Scribe is right, I should never leave your side!"

She smiled and they both entered the tent.

Chapter Ten~ Gemaia

That night, Pythagoras had agreed to visit Morvan, for a game of Gemaia. They sat on cushions in an ornately decorated room of Morvan's large house. Food and drink had been placed in front of them by Morvan's wife, Priori.

"It's been a long time, my rival," Pythagoras said.

"Too long," replied Morvan. "I always considered our rivalry when we were both students here in Egypt to be a challenge for both of us, it sharpened both of our wits."

"Yes, Morvan, that's certainly one way to put it." Pythagoras said. "You've been fortunate in having a lovely wife, Priori. She's held in high esteem I understand, as the Counselor to Eimon," Pythagoras added.

"She's only a woman," Morvan replied.

"Ah, yes, I remember that you always had the prettiest women around you Morvan, yet your attitude toward them was...condescending to say the least!"

"All women are the same, including I suspect your Theoclea," Morvan added.

Pythagoras smiled, "That is where you are dead wrong, Morvan. She is an extraordinary woman, the most powerful woman that I have ever met. I suspect that history may remember her as one of the most influential women of all time! My name and yours, Morvan will be forgotten-She will be remembered for all of the ages of the Earth!"

"Impressive, Pythagoras-but surely you will be remembered for your thoughts on music, and mathematics. I may be remembered for other writings as well!"

"We shall see Morvan-It will all be noted on the Akashic Record."

"Yes, of course-The Akashic Record," Morvan replied, "and now on with game-Gemaia!"

They both sat down on cushions on opposite sides of a low table with a board that contained black and white squares. There were 12 semi-precious gemstones in front of one side of the board, and the same number of stones, type and quality, were set on the opposite side. Both men took the game seriously, and silence was observed. The first moves were quickly made on both sides, and then both men settled in for the midgame, Neither one of them spoke, but the time elapsed between moves became longer and longer as each man tried to imagine the almost infinite number of possibilities that stretched forward in time.

Morvan made a move and then looked up at Pythagoras.

"I am looking forward to the speech that Theoclea is scheduled to make in front of the paws of the Sphinx. There will also be dancing by Eimon's troupe, and a spectacular fire entertainment near the Great Pyramid before the speech. It's shaping up to be quite an event, Pythagoras."

Pythagoras idly played with a wooden serpent that sat on a black square on the third row of the board. He touched it and paused, as if re-thinking the logic of the move. He stared at the board, and his hand went back to his chin. He then looked up at Morvan and said, "She's been working on this speech for a long time, I suspect, even before we knew of the trip to Egypt."

They maintained silence for a few minutes and studied the board.

"The children, said Morvan, "are they enjoying the trip?"

"Very much so, Morvan, they fancy themselves to be detectives, shrouded in mystery."

"Hah," said Morvan, "we all felt that way at their age!"

Pythagoras studied the board, "Your set doesn't contain the Crystal Lantern piece that is so popular in our Greek sets. Why is that, Morvan?"

Morvan sighed. "The few Crystal lanterns that we had have all stopped working since the last time that you were here, Pythagoras."

"Morvan, what do you know of the technology of the Crystal Lanterns?"

"Nothing, I've assumed that you, a scientist, a mathematician of all people must know the workings of those lamps!"

"No one knows the secret of the Crystal Lanterns, it's some kind of lost knowledge," Pythagoras said. "Perhaps a lost magic art that we cannot duplicate"

They both studied the board, and after a few more moves, and a lot of thought, they both toppled over their key pieces.

"It's a stalemate! The first stalemate that we have ever had," said Morvan.

Pythagoras smiled, "yes-obviously a stalemate."

"You've gotten better at this, Morvan," Pythagoras said. "Yes, I've gotten better at a lot of things," Morvan replied.

86

Morvan stood up and went over to a large cabinet.

"I still have the wand and staff that Azura made for me. He opened the cabinet, and took out a long box made of rare woods.

There were inlaid designs with symbols on them. He laid the box on a table and opened it. Inside of the box was a wand made of willow, with an obelisk crystal on the end, and a matching staff.

"Oh, how I remember this wand and staff. I saw you use it many times when we were students. I still have the wand of rosewood, with an egg-shaped crystal that Azura made for me, and the matching staff." Pythagoras said. "They're back in my tent. I always take them with me wherever I go."

"Perhaps we'll have a contest with the wands and staffs while you are here in Egypt," Morvan said.

"I think not, Morvan we have a lot to do as it is-perhaps another time."

Morvan then motioned to Pythagoras. "Come with me, there is a room that I want to show you!" He got up from his cushion and proceeded to take Pythagoras out to a hallway.

They met Priori, Morvan's wife in the hallway, and Morvan said to her, "Make sure that no one disturbs us, I want to show Pythagoras a few things." She looked at Pythagoras, then back at Morvan with a questioning look on her face. "Morvan, are you sure that..." He glared at her-"Just do as I say!" He said sternly.

She eyed him suspiciously, and finally said, "yes, I'll make sure that you are not disturbed," and she sighed, and moved on.

They walked down the hallway and turned to the right. There was an arch with ornate symbols on it and they went through. After that, there were many twists and turns, and other archways. Finally they came to a large wooden door, again with symbols on it. Morvan took out a large black key and opened the door-he motioned for Pythagoras to enter.

Pythagoras walked in, and what he saw was beyond his comprehension. There were shelves lined with what appeared to be books of a kind that he had never seen. They were encased in various animal skins. There were also glass front cases on a few tables. Pythagoras walked over and carefully looked at the books. The titles of most of them were on the back bindings of the books, most of which faced him. He looked at some of the titles-without saying a word, then he wandered over to the display cases. There were objects in the display cases the purpose of which he could only guess at.

Pythagoras continued to look around the room. "What is that device-over there, on the pedestal?"

"Ah, Pythagoras, that is a machine that talks, and makes music." They both walked over to the device.

"It is called a Leland-Arnaud Mark IV"

Pythagoras stared at it. It appeared to be an oak box with doors on the front. Attached to the back of the box was something that looked like a metal shoulder with part of an arm coming from the back. On the end of the arm was a circular piece with what appeared to be a metallic needle inserted into it. There was a circular table of some kind on the top of the box, and seated on the table was a black disc with minute grooves in it. Morvan took the disc off of the table, and showed it to Pythagoras. The disc had a hole in it, so that it could be seated on the table, which had a metal knob in the center of it.

"Pythagoras, this disc contains the sound of a voice singing, and strange music of the future. Do you see this red label around the hole in the middle? This writing tells you who made the disc, the name of the disc, and more information. This disc is called 'There'll be some changes made'. I can't read the writing of the future. The people who sent it to me said that the first sentences were, 'There'll be a change in the weather and a change in the sea, but most of all there'll be a change in me. My walk will be different, my talk and my name. Nothing about me is going to be the same'. That's all that I know about the music on this disc. You place the disc on the table, so that the hole in the middle fits properly, and then you turn this knob twenty times," Morvan indicated a knob and a lever on the side. "It's called a crank.'

He then turned the knob and lever twenty times, and the disc began to spin on the table. Morvan then took the 'arm' with the needle on the end, and inserted the needle into an outside groove on the end. He opened the doors in front of the box. For the next three minutes, Pythagoras stood there, not believing what he was hearing. A man's voice was singing. There were strange instruments all playing together-melodies and harmonies of a mode that he had never heard. As the music continued, the needle and its' arm moved closer and closer to the center. While the music was playing, Morvan opened and closed the doors in front of the oak box. When the doors were open the music was louder, and when they were closed the music was softer. After three minutes, the music stopped, and the needle went round and round the groove that was nearest to the center. Morvan took the needle off of the groove and moved the 'arm' back to its' resting place. He then touched a metal piece, and the table stopped spinning.

"Where was this made?" Pythagoras said.

"On a continent that we know nothing about-in the far future," Morvan replied.

"There'll be a change in the weather and a change in the sea, but after all, there'll be a change in me. My walk will be different, my talk and my name. Nothing about me is going to be the same."-you said that those were the first sentences. What do you think is the meaning of that ?" Pythagoras said.

"I don't know," replied Morvan.

"Perhaps it's a song about a prophecy, about transformation, or reincarnation," Pythagoras mused.

One particular object caught his attention. He stared at it, and then looked all around the room.

"The books and these objects, Morvan, they are all from the future!"

"Yes, Pythagoras, they are all 'relics' from the future!"

Pythagoras went over to the bookshelves. Most of the titles on the shelves were in languages that that he could not read, but some of them could be read.

"The Magister Mysterium," he said, as he touched one of the books. He saw another title, it said, in gold letters 'The Hermetarcanum of Theoclydes'. He perused other titles as they both stood in the room in silence. He then went over to the display case, and stared at the object that had fascinated him.

"How did you get all of these-'relics', Morvan?"

Morvan replied, "I discovered that things could be moved through time both forward and backward, if you know the right magic! There has to be, of course, a person, or group of people in the future that are willing to work with you."

"The 'relics' as you call them, Morvan-the group in the future, they don't just send them to you-you must send something in return to them-am I right Morvan?"

"Yes , Pythagoras, I must admit, that I send them objects that have been dug up from around the Holy Sites-there are thousands of objects-even the children find them. The people of the future find them to be valuable."

"So, Morvan, you are trading in precious 'relics', that are sent back and forth through time. Don't you find this to be immoral and unethical? It certainly goes against what we were taught!"

"Not necessarily, Pythagoras, there are no laws against trading in objects that one finds here. Sometimes, as a courtesy, I pay a local official, if I find something of great value. Look, Pythagoras, we are both considered to be High Priests of Egypt. That was our training. As High Priests, we, of all people, are expected to search for historic 'relics', we are the ones whose duty it is to add to the knowledge of Egypt's history. No one would question it if you, Pythagoras were to do some digging and searching during your stay here. If you find something, and want to take it with you, it's a common courtesy to pay a local official. I, for one, would expect you to do some searching-you of all people would know where to look, and could contribute much to history,"

"What is the name of this group that you are dealing with in the future, Morvan?"

"They're called 'The Antiquarian Brotherhood', a most noble name, I can assure you," replied Morvan. "They're a group that has been active in the far future for at least a thousand years, under different names and in different places…they have chapters all over the world. The group that I deal with is based in Cairo, in the far future."

Pythagoras looked all about the room, there was something here, he could feel it. Then, he saw the three crystals lying on a shelf. He walked over and looked at them. There was an Obelisk, a Tetrahedron, and a Pentagon.

"Morvan, what are you using these for? In our studies, we were cautioned against using these in a certain way-The triangle casting using these stones is the Triangle of Destruction-a triangle that causes disruption in the Acausal Realm.-it destroys forms and creates others-it is highly unstable. Have you been casting the Triangle of Destruction in order to send and receive these relics?"

"Well, yes, Pythagoras. I know how to use it. It can be used responsibly, with the right controls and Magic. "

"Morvan, that is completely against what we were taught!"

Pythagoras' attention went back to the display case. He pointed at the object that had fascinated him.

"What is that object, Morvan, and what is its' purpose?"

"Ah," said Morvan, "that is the prize of my collection! It is a weapon from the future!"

He opened the display case and held the 'weapon' up. He found a box in the case and opened it to reveal small metal balls.

"You pull on this lever, and put the metal balls into the slots-you have to pull the lever for each metal ball that you put into this part- and the long part is called the barrel. They explained that to me.

The lever is called a wedge. Once all of the metal balls are 'loaded in', it is ready to be used. You just have to pull back this part, and it is ready.

"What is it, Morvan?" Pythagoras asked.

"It is called a Colt Pocket Model, with a date of 1849, with a ramrod wedge-It has a six inch barrel, and it will be used in a civil war of the far future, on a continent that we know nothing about-it fires the metal balls at people. The six balls can be fired in quick succession. All that you have to do is pull back this piece, and you're ready to fire it again.

"Did they explain to you how to reload those chambers?" asked Pythagoras.

"They explained it to me, but I haven't tried to reload it, yet. There may be other things that they have to send..." Morvan replied. When I received it, it was loaded, and all six balls were in place. I've tried it four times on a target, and it has incredible accuracy. It is a weapon of immense power, against which we, of this time have no known defense. It is called a *gun*, specifically a *revolver*, Pythagoras."

"A *gun*, you say," Morvan.

"Yes, Pythagoras, a *gun*," Morvan replied

Chapter Eleven... The Scribe and the Healing

The Scribe had been fasting, and he was eager to try the healing as he opened the flap of the tent and let Pythagoras and Theoclea in. Pythagoras had brought a drum, and everyone then seated themselves on cushions. They meditated in quiet for a few minutes. Pythagoras then performed a 'casting' of a triangle of Healing and Protection, using three crystals that were in his pocket. They were all of matching transparency, color and size. One was a five-pointed star, the other was a sphere, and a third one was egg shaped.

He took out his star-shaped crystal and held it high as if absorbing its' energy, then placed it in one part of the edge of the tent. He whispered some words, one of which was 'past'. Pythagoras walked over to the opposite side of the tent and seemed to be drawing energy from the star. He took out a spherical-shaped crystal, and placed it against the tent wall. Pythagoras seemed to be drawing energy from the star to the sphere, and whispered some words, one of which was 'present'.

Pythagoras walked to the side of the tent opposite the doorway and placed his egg-shaped crystal against the tent wall, whispering some words, one of which was 'future', then walked back to the Star and said something to it.

"Now we're ready," he said the Triangle has been been cast.They all sat inside of the triangle. Then the healing began.

Pythagoras started by drumming a slow heartbeat. Theoclea put a glass of the liquid in The Scribe's hand. She was sitting on a cushion very close to The Scribe, facing him. "Here," she said-"drink this liquid." He drank it, and then put the glass down. She then gave him a vial of the oil and said "place the oil under your eyes, wait for it to penetrate, then do that twice more." He did what he asked her to do, and then handed the vial back to her. She put the vial away in a box, and then stood up and walked behind the Scribe.

She nodded to Pythagoras to speed up the heartbeat. She placed her hands on his eyes and began to share her Aura with his. She whispered to him, "The liquid and the oil come from the Himalaya mountains. There is a woman that I know named Premavati, and she has come to see me during the past nine months. She's from the Himalayas, far to the East of here, and she makes these oils and liquids. She has also shared some words of magic with me." Theoclea started to chant:

> "From ignorance, lead me to truth-
> From darkness, lead me to light-
>
> From death, lead me to immortality
>
> Aum... peace, peace, peace."

Over and over she chanted. Each time the chant got louder, and she nodded to Pythagoras to increase the speed of the drumming. She persisted in this for perhaps ten minutes more. The energy that was surging through her became more and more intense, and it was being transferred to the Scribe through her aura. The Triangle also intensified the force and energy behind the healing. Finally she ended the chant and shouted "Aum, peace, peace, peace!"

Pythagoras immediately stopped drumming.

She took her hands away from his eyes, and told him to keep his eyes closed.

Theoclea walked around and sat on the cushion facing him. She took out two gemstones from a pouch and touched them gently to his eyes.
Then she said,

"May the strength of your eyes
Be restored as before
May the power of your thoughts
Reveal all your lives, and more!
The spell is cast the work is done
With newfound vision you'll see
The Light of the Sun!"
She took the stones away-
"Open your eyes!" she said

He slowly opened his eyes, and exclaimed-"I can see, I can see! He looked around the room, slowly turning his head to the right. Then he turned back to the left and saw Pythagoras-

"Pythagoras! I can see you! I can see all of the things in this tent! His head turned slightly to the left and he saw Theoclea in front of him. He stared at her eyes, and exclaimed "I can see you, Theoclea! He looked slowly to the left, and said "I see everything. I had forgotten the shapes, the colors in the tent. His eyes wandered back to Theoclea. "Theoclea, I can see you." He stood up and walked toward her, finally putting his hands on either side of her face.

There were tears in his eyes, "I can see you, and I have seen you before! I saw you on Atlantis!" He looked over at Pythagoras-"and you were there too, Pythagoras, on Atlantis! It's slowly all coming back to me!"

He turned and walked toward the tent flap, walked outside, and looked all around. They followed him outside. He stared into the middle distance, and saw The Sphinx and the Pyramids nearby. "I can see The Sphinx, I remember more clearly now. So many years ago-the carving of the face looking down at the ground-and yet-I still don't remember my most recent incarnations." He turned toward Pythagoras and Theoclea, and said, "I remember your book."

He went back to the tent, and emerged with a piece of parchment and a writing instrument. "I'll write all of this down for you! I know where it is-it's in the Great Pyramid. There is a faint white line that starts at the bottom of one side. You can barely see it, but it rises seven degrees as it winds around the Pyramid, all the way to the top. You can see it best in the very early morning.

"Measure eight feet in from the start of the line at the base of the Pyramid. Then measure four feet up. You will

101

have to remove that block and some of the blocks around it. You will need Vorios' help in removing the blocks, for they are very heavy. He has not shown you all of his magic. I seem to remember something about Vorios, but it is still vague. My memory of my time on Atlantis is still as vague as my memory of the incarnations of the last two thousand years, but I seem to know that Vorios can work the magic. Tomb robbers do not know this, but there is an internal ramp that was used to build the Great Pyramid. The internal ramp never intersected the other passageways, or the King and Queen's chamber. There were other Pyramids that were built with internal ramps, the 'Sun' temple, for instance, that is in another location."

"When you remove the blocks you will be able to get inside. There is a narrow tunnel there and it ends ten feet inside the pyramid to reveal an internal ramp. Turn to your right and walk another fifteen feet, or so, and you'll see a symbol of three intersecting circles, or crystals…it's about three or four feet up on the left. The rock plate there is thick and cannot easily be removed. Once again, you will need Vorios' magic to remove it! The book is behind it!"

"It may be difficult- Hemiunu told me that a special mortar was put there. You'll find these things easily now, because the limestone has been eroded. Hemiunu told me how to get into the passageway, and I was the one who hid the book. I realized that the book contained ideas that could be of great benefit to mankind, or create great destruction. At that time I had my own magical secrets and tools. The book was useless without the first volume-but Pythagoras, you say that you have the first volume! I hope that the book is still there. I don't think that tomb robbers have discovered the internal ramp. They have entered the King and Queen's chambers and have taken a lot of the treasure, but the internal ramp is almost impossible to find."

He had been writing as he was talking, and gave the design of the plan to Pythagoras.

He looked down once more, and then faced Theoclea. "Once again, Theoclea, tell me how long this will last."

"Perhaps only a few days, a week at the most. Your memory may improve even more in the next day. You may lose your sight suddenly, within a few minutes. Your memory will continue to improve even after your sight starts to fail-you may have a few more minutes of improved memory-even a last revelation, and then all will return to its previous state before the healing."

He turned, hugged her again, and kissed her on both cheeks. Tears appeared in his eyes once more.

"You have given me my sight and memory back-I have never received a finer gift from anyone, no matter how much time it lasts." He turned to Pythagoras, and said,

"You must gather the tools together and look for the book as soon as possible. It will have to be after Theoclea gives the Speech. Vorios must go with you." Then he turned to Theoclea.

"I think that it would be wise for the children to go on this quest as well. They may have an easier time getting through the ramp if it is covered with debris." Theoclea nodded her head in agreement

"I know," she said.

Pythagoras went into the tent, took down the Triangle of Healing and Protection and then emerged. They all hugged each other, and said their goodbyes for the day.

"Good luck," the Scribe shouted after they had walked some distance. He continued to look around. "If only I could remember more," he thought.

They walked some distance, and then, Pythagoras turned to Theoclea and said,

"The Scribe...he is a reincarnation of 'The Grandfather' from Atlantis, am I right?"

"Yes, and others," she said quietly. They walked on.

Pythagoras decided on the way back, that the next day, they would gather the tools together, and make their plans based on the Scribes' information. Theoclea was going to have private meetings with Eimon, Priori, and Miriam. In the evening Eimon had prepared a special feast and dance event for Theoclea's entourage. They would look for the book and the internal ramp in the Great Pyramid sometime after Theoclea's Speech.

Chapter Twelve... The meeting with Eimon, Priori, and Miriam in the morning.

In the morning, Theoclea met with Eimon, Priori, and Miriam. They were private meetings, spaced one hour apart, with time for Theoclea to meditate between the conversations.

First, Theoclea met with Eimon. Eimon came into the tent, and sat down on a cushion, facing Theoclea, whose eyes were closed, deep in meditation. Theoclea opened her eyes, and smiled broadly at Eimon. Formal salutations were exchanged, and then Theoclea said,

"Eimon, I'm going to ask you to reveal a secret to me! I'd like to know the entire process that you go through, and all of the ingredients needed to make your hair that brilliant shade of red!"

Eimon laughed, "They told me that you might be full of surprises, and they were right!"

"Theoclea, there is a woman who has taught me how to do it. She comes to the Royal Court once or twice a year. She's from the Himalaya mountains, and her name is Premavati!"

"Premavati," Theoclea said, "I know her! She has been to Delphi, and I've bought healing potions, and oils from her. I've learned much from her, and we've had conversations about many things. She never mentioned to me that she knew how to change the color of my hair!"

"Perhaps, you never asked her," Eimon said. Theoclea thought about this for a few moments.

"You're right, it was something that was never mentioned, it just didn't come up. Okay, then what's the secret?" Theoclea said.

Eimon laughed again. "First, you must ask Premavati to provide you with a special jar of powder that only comes from the area near the islands of Sumatra, and Java!"

"That's where the clay came from that was used to make my Rose Medallion! It must be the same clay, but in a powdered form!" Theoclea took out the Rose Medallion from the pouch in front of her, and showed it to Eimon. They briefly discussed its' use. Then Eimon said,

"Perhaps it is the same clay, Theoclea, I wouldn't know about that part. Premavati sells powdered henna, and a different kind of paste."

"She mixes the powdered red clay, the henna, and the paste together, and lathers up my hair. I leave it on for a certain amount of time, then wash my hair, and, it's red!"

"The next time that Premavati comes to Delphi I shall ask her...about this," Theoclea said. Other matters were discussed, and then Eimon left. Theoclea put the Medallion back in its' pouch.

Priori came in next. She sat down on the cushion, facing Theoclea, whose eyes were once again closed, deep in meditation. Theoclea then opened her eyes, and looked seriously into Priori's eyes. Once again, formal salutations were exchanged, and then Theoclea said,

"I have only said what I am about to say to you, to one other person. I met him during the time that the story of Atlantis was being revealed to me. His name was Avram, and he was the next in command to an evil man named Davros. Davros was a descendant of 'The Sons of Belial', a group of ruthless warriors that lived on

Atlantis. I was abducted from the Temple of Delphi by magical means, and drugged as well. When I came back to consciousness, my hands were bound behind me. I won't tell you all of the details, but through the revelations of my visions, I slowly gained the respect of Avram, and shocked Davros. When Avram took me back to the room where I was being held, I asked him along the way why he was following Davros. He told me that he was a soldier, and it was his duty to obey orders. I told him what I am about to tell you."

"Remember Priori, you are a free soul. Do not follow him in the end. You will know when the time is right, and you will know what to do!"

Theoclea took out the Rose Medallion, showed it to Priori, and explained its' use. This was followed by a few moments of silence, and Priori said, "Theoclea, you are the most remarkable woman that I have ever met. Thank you for showing me the Medallion. I shall ponder all that you have said to me." She bowed to Theoclea, and then left.

Theoclea returned to her meditations, and put the Medallion back in its' pouch. Miriam came in next. She sat down on the cushion, facing Theoclea, whose eyes were once again closed, deep in meditation. Theoclea opened her eyes, and Miriam saw that there were tears in them.

Once again, formal salutations were exchanged, and then Theoclea said,

"Miriam, what do you know of the Medallion that you are guarding?"

Miriam looked down at the gold colored bag that she always wore, and said,

"My father told me that it was a priceless treasure. He told me that it was rare, and said that there were only three others that had been made. He predicted that I might meet someone one day of very high spiritual stature, and that I could only discuss the Medallion with that person, You are the one in my father's prediction, Theoclea."

Theoclea nodded, she reached down for the pouch that was in front of her, and took out the Rose Medallion. She showed the face side to Miriam. "No doubt you know that the face on the Rose Medallion is the face of Inanna, one of the first Goddesses. Her symbol was 'The Rose'."

"Miriam, show me your Medallion, and hold it exactly the way that I am holding mine. Miriam reached into the gold pouch, and took out the Medallion with

Axcelotl's face on it. She held it in the way that Theoclea had indicated.

Suddenly, there were three flashes of light that travelled quickly from Axcelotl's Medallion to the Rose Medallion. "The medallions are now linked," Theoclea said. "Miriam, what else did your father tell you about your medallion?"

"He told me that it was a divination tool of some kind, and that I would learn how to use it. He didn't know anything about the woman whose face was depicted on the Medallion, but he told me to guard it with my life! He said that it was one of the greatest treasures in the world, and that it was priceless. I have learned how to use it, but many times I don't understand what I am seeing when I turn it over."

"Miriam, I often see the words of poets of the past, present, and future, on the Medallion, but you know that the right words at the right time are expected of me. Other people see other things. Do you know that I used the Rose Medallion during my speech to the pilgrims at Eleusis?"

"Yes," Miriam said. "I have read your speech, and I would to have been there to hear you speak the words, and see the magic that took place. They say that a phoenix appeared in the sky, and that two lightning bolts crossed each other under a cloud making your sign of the Delphic Oracle. It must have been very exciting." Theoclea looked down at the ground, and then said. "To this day, I don't know the source of that magic, I may never know where it came from!"

"I will tell you about the face on your Medallion, Miriam. It's the face of Axcelotl wearing the crown of the three Crystals. She was the last queen of Atlantis. She was my Ancient Mother, and I was the child. I won't tell you the whole story-but I will tell you this. There was a group of ruthless warriors on Atlantis called 'The Sons of Belial'. There was also a peaceful group on Atlantis, called 'The Children of the Law of One'. They wanted to use the crystal energy of Atlantis for communications, heating their homes, and powering their ships. There was a third group that held the secret of the crystal power, and they were called the Crystal Ones. They often intervened between the hostility occurred between the other two groups."

"Axcelotl was the leader of 'the Crystal Ones', and she was the Last Queen of Atlantis. The medallion that you have belonged to her. It has always been assumed that the medallion was lost when Atlantis was engulphed by the sea during the great catastrophe nine thousand years ago."

She told Miriam the rest of the story of Axcelotl, and some of the details of the adventure on Atlantis. They meditated for awhile. *'I must tell Pythagoras and Vorios not to keep their medallions on their persons. They must lock them up, and two of our men must guard the tents. All four medallions must not be together in the same room,' Theoclea thought.*

Afer they had meditated, they hugged each other. They then said their goodbyes. Theoclea said, "Don't ever let the medallion out of your sight. Your father was right, guard it with your life!"

Chapter Thirteen... The Dream, the vision, and the Reading

Later the same day in the afternoon, after Pythagoras left, Theoclea stared at the ceiling of the tent. She imagined that she saw-

"the nude women,

statues,

skeletons and chiefs,

puppets and priests"

of Pythagoras' poem.

She had the poem next to her, she read it, then stared at

the ceiling once again, and thought that she saw

"the great beasts with their trunks held high,

squirting water on the children

who lived in the East"

Then sleep took her into another realm. She saw herself sitting on the Tripod chair, the whispers of the dragon's breath seeping up through the two cracks that crossed in the floor under the chair. The Psephoi stones rattled in their bowl. The Oomphalos stone was nearby, and there was the smell of laurel.

Gently, she fell into a trance. She suddenly felt the familiar feeling of being frozen in a frame of black and white film, as if it had gotten stuck in an old projector.

She was in a dark cave of some kind-she saw her children, frozen in the frame, Pythagoras was there, as well as someone else. There was a flickering of light, on and off, on the cave wall. Just as her eyes were adjusting to the dark, the room became a room that seemed familiar. Yes, it was the inside of the Great Hall of the Temple in the Sand on Atlantis, before the destruction over 9000 years before. Color returned to the scene. Just red and gold at first-she saw Axcelotl sitting on the throne, with Aura the dancer, on one side of her, and Sonja, the singer on the other side. Axcelotl smiled, and suddenly the room was flooded with light, and images appeared on three of the walls.

The images were recognizable, all thirty images of the KeyRose set flashed by quickly in random order-the red, gold and black keys added to the image event.

There were pictures of three of the medallions as well as images of the KeyRose boxes with various designs on them, and the Pentacle and Rose symbol as well. There were other images that were not recognizable. They swirled, and went by quickly, flashing on all three walls. There was also strange music in the background. It was the music in Pythagoras' poem-

"Instruments that made
a dub-dub sound
dub-dub, step-step
crunching all around,
in a myriad of beats
a cacophony of sound.
The music encircled me
going round and round!"

The images and music started to slow down. In a flash, she saw a woman who seemed to be in another chamber of the same Temple , on Atlantis-in the distant past. She looked somewhat like Theoclea-dressed in the red, black and gold. The woman sat on a tripod chair, yet there was no dragon's breath, no cracks under the chair, and the images were still playing on the walls. The music died down, but continued at a slower pace-the image event continued to slow down. The woman on the chair seemed to be in a trance induced by the images and sounds. Indeed, she was in another room of the Temple in the Sand, for there were large crystals all around. It was an altar room of some kind.

The woman came out of her trance, and looked in Theoclea's direction. She spoke, gently, with a soothing voice.

"This is my prophecy for you, Theoclea." Suddenly, the scene changed again, and Theoclea was in another room, in another time-in the far future.

She sat on one of the chairs that she had seen people of the future use- chairs that could be folded and placed against walls. She faced an audience of six people. There were three women on one side, and three men on another side, and they were dressed in the clothes of the future, clothing that she seen before. Each one held a KeyRose piece in their hands, as well as a paper to read. There was a seventh person-a man in the back who sat away from the others. He was sitting in a comfortable chair and held a pipe that seemed to be emitting smoke. Every once in a while, he inhaled the smoke.

He also had a writing instrument, and what appeared to be a sheaf of many leaves of writing paper bound together. He said,

"Theoclea, today you are the Solitaire, what is the problem?"

Theoclea thought for a moment, and said-

"I seem to have lost the main purpose of my mission-I seek clarity on this."

The man in the back pointed to one of the women and said-"Rose?"

Rose looked at Theoclea, and then at her paper.

"I have randomly chosen a piece from the KeyRose, Theoclea and it is the Ancient Mother. On this paper there are questions that I should ask you, for I am playing the part of the Ancient Mother-I will ask this question-it comes from the poem that you know so well.

What do you see, Theoclea?"

"Moonlit mirth, infinity?
The past, the future,
The shore at night-
all are part of your
luminous sight-or
perhaps you see the verdant
plain,
the lake of gloom."

"What do you see, Theoclea?"

Theoclea sighed.

119

"I see that I have taken a vow to take on the realization of another person's dream...Orpheus. Yet, I am confused and afraid. I fear for my loved ones. It's as if one key piece of the puzzle is missing."

One of the men raised his hand. The man in the back recognized a "Rudolph."

"I have been given the role and piece that shows the Fingerprint. One of the questions on my sheet seems appropriate-What keeps you from going ahead and seeing this through to its' final conclusion? You know the Fingerprint poem well." He read the poem-

THE FINGERPRINT

She left a fingerprint
on the Gate
It took so long to get so near
Now YOU are here,
Why hesitate?
For most of us the path is clear
Now why stand still when you've come so far?
Your strength and will
Tell us who you are.

Ah, yes this Gate may be your last,
and you are filled with fear, of course
GO THROUGH!
The stones have all been cast,
this Gate will lead you to the Source!

"Theoclea, have you told us the whole truth, what are you really afraid of?"

Theoclea's eyes welled up with tears, she looked down for a few moments, and then said-

"I'm afraid-for my loved ones, for in a vision, I have seen a weapon of the future-a terrible weapon-and there is no known defense against it! It is going to be used against me. Someone is going to die, maybe more than one person!"

There was hush that filled the room as they all looked at each other, and at the man in the back. Theoclea sat there-she closed her eyes. She was in tears. The man in the back recognized four others. Each had a KeyRose piece chosen at random. Each one asked Theoclea a question, and she responded. In the end, all had spoken. Then, each one in turn, playing the characters on their KeyRose pieces offered something positive for her to ponder. The man in the back took a puff of smoke, then blew it out and said,

121

"I am just the facilitator here, Theoclea, my name is Carl. What positive feeling can you come away with here-you have heard the words of the Tribal Council.

Theoclea once again looked down, and she heard a whispered voice say 'It was there from the very beginning'. She pondered this and looked around to see where the voice came from- she saw amorphous lights flickering in a night sky- the scene was frozen, as if... and then...a realization dramatically came to her...She blurted out-

"Yes, of course, it was there from the very beginning, and I failed to recognize it!-The projector-It's starting." She turned to the others and said, once more, "It's starting!" She looked at the man in the back of the room and said-"Carl-It's Starting!" She pondered this, and then she responded forcefully.

"I think that I know what the missing piece of the puzzle is-I will know what to do when the time comes-There were women like me in the Temple in the Sand, and there were image projectors-and... I see my mission more clearly now, and I will bring it to its' inevitable conclusion. There were others like me in the past. Not all of them had the Dragon's breath in the subterranean chamber-for many of the ancient ones, images and sounds put them in a trance-they are my Ancient sisters, and Axcelotl is my Ancient Mother! I thank you, one and all."

With that, the dream ended and Theoclea slowly made her way out of sleep and back to her part of the tent along the Nile. She turned over, and saw that her KeyRose box lay beside her-it was open, and the six pieces of her vision were placed in front of the box."

She thought 'I can tell no one of this dream. *I see, I hear…the whispers'.*

That evening, Theoclea's entourage enjoyed the special feast that Eimon had prepared in a special tent, that was followed by a special dance that Eimon had prepared for them. The dance was in the special Egyptian style that was currently in favor, and ended with a wild, passionate display that was full of comedy and laughter. Theoclea was thrilled, walked up and hugged all of the dancers.

Chapter Fourteen... The Parade and the Fire Entertainment

The following day was a day of rest, and meditation for Theoclea. The speech would be given in the evening, but Theoclea was not to be a part of the parade, and the fire entertainment that was the prelude to the speech. It was decided that it would be too dangerous for her to attend. Theoclea insisted that Vorios take the children on the parade route, so that they could see all of it.

Eimon and two members of her dance troupe were at the head of the parade. Eimon, with her red hair, was the dancer in the middle, and it won't come as a surprise to you that one of the other dancers had dark hair, and the third one had light, blond hair. The plan was, that when the parade reached the Great Pyramid of Giza, and the fire entertainment started, Eimon would move on to the Sphinx, and make sure that everything was to Theoclea, Morain and Panelle's liking, and that all the preparations were being put in place for Theoclea's speech.

Egyptian dancing was very different, in that period, from the style represented by Bella, and the Bella-Festa troupe of Greece.

The Egyptian dancing had a wild, passionate quality to it, and there was an element of comedy and theatricality that one would not find in Greece, where refined hand movements, epitomized by Bella's style were the hallmark.

Eimon was a great 'comedic' dancer. That, in itself involved a keen sense of timing, and a knowledge of the dance moves and costuming that were needed to achieve this. The three women used spinning and 'big skirt moves' that were somewhat reminiscent of a 'Zar'. The public, of course, knew that this was not a 'Zar', for the 'Zar' was a healing dance, known only to the initiates, and not performed publically. The dancers only pretended to be in a trance, and occasionally would bump each other out of the way, pretending to claim the spotlight.

There were spins, controlled by strong crossover movements, for the three of them were known to be the finest dancers in all of Egypt. They touched their skirts as they danced, something not often done in Greece. Pointed toe movements, swift head turns, and intricate body tilting were used, always interspersed with comedic jealous glances, and attempts to steal the spotlight from one or both of the other dancers. Sometimes they would pretend to be angry at one another and chase each other around in a circle, only to return and execute intricate back and forth patterns.

The public loved this. It was estimated that thousands upon thousands of people lined the parade route that stretched from the outskirts of Cairo to the Giza Plateau. As Eimon and her dancers performed, intricate arm placements, and foot slides changed the look of each turn. Skirt flips, achieved by a deceptively difficult control of hips, body, and heels added to the fun. It looked so easy, yet was innately well controlled, planned, and practiced. For the occasion, the dancers used the red, gold and black colors of the Delphic Oracle, to honor her. They all had tattoos, and wore silver jewelry and other ornaments. The dancers were accompanied by two drummers carrying different sized 'djembes'. They performed at various spots along the parade route, followed by other entertainers, jugglers, and floats of various kinds.

The parade was reminiscent of lines from Pythagoras' poetry:

There were Magicians, and Puppeteers,
Priestesses and Priests,
Lions standing high on stilts,
Chieftains, and Chiefs,
While on the floats,
there were statues
of the
great beasts from the East
with their trunks held high
squirting water at the sky.
In a fine display of water play
That will not be equaled until the day
When the pond and the tree
have had their final say...
(There were women in strange clothing and the Goddess of the
night.
While a full moon waxed and waned
by a flock of crows in flight...)

Finally, the dancers, led by Eimon performed their entire dance to a joyful appreciative crowd in front of the great Pyramid of Giza. The crowd had swelled along the parade route to perhaps more than a hundred

128

thousand people, and the Heralds had set up ten huge screens on either side of the Pyramid, that allowed all to see and hear the events as they unfolded. After the dancing had finished, Eimon left, to join Theoclea and the others in front of the Sphinx.

Then, one of the Heralds appeared in front of the Pyramid, and made a universal sign for quiet that was seen and respected by all. A hush fell over the crowd, they all knew what was coming...It was time for Skyfire, Karma-'The Moonchild', and their troupe 'The Cairo Fire Brigade' to perform.

A tent had been set up in front of the Giza Pyramid with the sign of a huge flame on the side-'The Cairo Fire Brigade' emblem.

Total silence was observed, out of respect for the dangerous nature of their performance, and their love for the chief of the Tribe, 'Skyfire', an internationally known performer. Here again, comedy was joined to expertise, producing a high order of excitement-seemingly wild, like Eimon's dancing, yet fully planned and under control. The tent flap opened, and 'Skyfire' appeared first. He was tall, and was dressed like a clown, with an oversized red 'fez' hat, white powder on his face, and black charcoal around his eyes and mouth. Unnoticed, about twenty feet on either side of him were the 'safeties' ready for any mishaps. They were dressed in black and had water, and towels- they skillfully blended into the night, and were completely unnoticed by the crowd. 'Skyfire', wore a multi-colored shirt of red, black and gold for the occasion that appeared to be tattered-but was purposely made to look so. He wore white pantaloons and no shoes. All of his clothing was made of cotton-it was the only material used in the Cairo Fire Brigade's clothing.

He bowed to the crowd, and said "Are you ready for some fire?" They roared back, "Yes!" He turned around and looked disgusted, then turned back to them and smiled.

"I CAN'T HEAR YOU. I SAID ARE YOU READY FOR SOME FIRE?"

"YES! They shouted. He smiled.

"ARE YOU READY TO BURN?" he shouted. Once again, they roared back "YES!"

"THEN LET THE FIRE, AND THE BURN, BEGIN!" he shouted!

He took a swig from what appeared to be a large wine bottle, and, picking up a torch from the ground that had been carefully placed there in a tube, he held the torch high, and held it close to his mouth. He then blew the flame-the fire emerged from his mouth and shot up at least thirty feet into the air, where it dispersed "NOW THAT'S A FINE WINE, AND A FINE FLAME," he shouted, pretending to be somewhat intoxicated. Everyone could see and hear him because of the Herald's magic.

"More, More, More!" The crowd chanted.

He took a larger swig from the large wine bottle, held the torch high, and brought it close to his mouth. He then blew the flame-the fire emerged from his mouth and shot up at least thirty feet into the air, and then climbed higher-to sixty feet. It then dispersed. The crowd roared. He then had his men bring out an Obelisk that had a sign on it. The sign said...'

'One hundred feet...The World record...won by 'Skyfire'. He looked at it and shrugged. "That's nothing, wait until you see what's going to happen tonight," he said, as he smiled at the crowd.

"ARE YOU READY, FOR THIS?"

"YES!" said the crowd. He turned around, once more pretending to be dejected and disgusted. Then he turned to them again, and said,

"I CAN'T HEAR YOU, I SAID
ARE YOU READY FOR THIS?"

"YES!" said the crowd, once again, even louder.

131

He took a larger swig from the large wine bottle, held the torch high, and once again brought it close to his mouth. He blew the flame-the fire emerged from his mouth and shot up at least sixty feet into the air, and then climbed higher-to ninety, a hundred, and a hundred and ten feet. He had beaten his own World Record. The crowd roared.

He pretended to be intoxicated, and quieted them down. "I'll be back," he said,

"You ain't seen nothin' yet. I need a rest, before I try it again!"

As he walked back to the tent, three large canisters were brought out and placed at least ten feet apart. They looked like large oil lamps and their light lit up the performance area. 'Skyfire' then turned around, and said, "Here's Karma and the rest of the Brigade to entertain you..." He walked over to a hammock in front of the tent, jumped into it, and pretended to doze off. At a precise moment the three canisters shot flames, ten to twenty feet high, Each one seemed to have a metal flute supporting the flame, and different musical tones came out as the three fountains of flame shot the flames higher and lower. It was a melody in flame, the entrance music for Karma. There was also a group of drummers accompanying the singing flames.

Karma and another woman came out with hoops-there were half a dozen balls attached to each hoop, and the balls were deftly lit by torches held by the women. The torches were then placed in tubes in the ground. The women then began to dance with the twirling spinning hoops, with their fiery balls whirling around them. One could hear the signature whoosh of the flames. The dancing was similar to Eimon's dancing, passionate, and wild, except that the women wore minimal costumes-skimpy tops and bottoms that were worn as much for safety as for theatricality.

The women's hoop dancing with the flaming balls, was followed by two tattooed men who staged a mock battle with flaming swords, much to the crowd's delight. Then, a huge man came out of the tent, and appeared to be holding two heavy chains. He walked around, and slapped the chains on the ground. Each time that he did this multicolored flames appeared on the ground accompanied by popping firecracker noises. The huge man went back to the tent, and the flame canisters changed to a slower melody.

Finally, two jugglers appeared, each one juggled three burning torches, the torches rose higher and higher, and then the men proceeded to step back, away from each other, and juggle the torches back and forth.

133

The crowd applauded. When they were finished, they each walked around to a different adjacent side of the pyramid, so that they both could be seen. Each man was handed a larger torch by one of the 'safeties'.

'Skyfire' seemed to have awakened from his 'nap' in the hammock, walked forward to the edge of two of the sides, and quieted the crowd once more.

A hush once more fell over the crowd.

They could see Skyfire and the men far off to the right and left of him.

"We have imported the finest wine from Greece, to attempt this. It was given to me as a gift by Theoclea. I am told that it is over one hundred years old and has been kept in a cellar in the Temple of Delphi just for an occasion such as this! He smacked his lips, and held up a large bottle in a unique Greek design, the crowd roared. He quieted them. " I do this to honor a woman who made a prediction to my parents before I was born."

"Theoclea said to my parents that-

"The flame of this child's passion for his art, will be known all over the world," and Theoclea's prophecy has come true!"

There were tears in his eyes, and he brought out a handkerchief, dried his eyes, and then took on an uncharacteristically serious expression. A heartbeat started on a drum.

He saw the two jugglers standing on either side of two adjacent sides of the Pyramid,

He asked the crowd for quiet. The drummer's heartbeat was very quiet.

"Please be patient, this is very dangerous."

He raised his right arm, and pointed to the very top of the Pyramid. The Giza Pyramid-The Great Pyramid of Khufu-

The tallest building on earth-four hundred and eighty feet high. No higher building would be built for another twenty three hundred years. It would be called the 'Eiffel Tower'.

He held the Greek wine bottle up and took a swig that seemed to last forever, then he held the torch to his mouth and blew the fire-the flame rose up to one hundred feet-then to two hundred-he kept blowing-he had beat his own world record-then to three hundred-he kept blowing-then, without losing force to four hundred. His breath seemed to be limitless. Climbing steadily the flame started to stall at four hundred and fifty, but then gained momentum- four hundred sixty-seventy-and finally four hundred and eighty feet, and still climbing. When it hit five hundred feet, it rose higher, and then, the flame burst into a white incandescent cloud that continued to rise.

'Skyfire' held the bottle, tears in his eyes, he placed it on the ground, and then he turned and looked at the jugglers. Each one held one large burning torch. He had asked Theoclea's entourage to bring the torches from Greece, and had told the head of the Greek Heralds where to get them. The Egyptian Priests had then blessed the torches in a proscribed manner. The jugglers had been personally chosen by him. The crowd, of course, was cheering wildly and the heartbeat drumming was louder. He turned and motioned to the crowd,

"It's not over yet," he said, trying to quiet them down. A respectful hush came over the crowd. Both jugglers had been chosen because they had won medals in the discus throw and similar events at the Greek Olympic Games. He had met them in Greece, and asked them to join his troupe. He had personally trained them, and motioned to both of them. They started to whirl around faster and faster-the signature whoosh of the fire could still be heard above the crowd noise due to the Herald's magic. They whirled the torches round and round, gaining energy with each revolution. 'Skyfire' saw that they were close to letting go, but he was listening to the 'whoosh of the fire'. The sound had to be just right. When the moment was right, he looked up at the incandescent cloud, and then pointed simultaneously at both of them. They hurled their torches high into the air. The torches sailed up to one hundred, two hundred, three hundred, four hundred feet, and seemingly without losing momentum, they sailed over the four hundred and eighty foot mark of the point of the Pyramid- then beyond to five hundred, and higher until they crossed under the cloud, and then continued down. As they descended they burned out, and each one was then caught by the juggler on the other side of the Pyramid.

Loudly, 'Skyfire' said, "The Sign of the Delphic Oracle, our homage to the great woman who will speak to us his evening."

The crowd cheered. He usually ended his performances with a laugh, and he was able to quiet them down again. His expression remained serious though.

"My mother took me to see Theoclea after I was born, and asked Theoclea once more about my prospects, and these are the words that Theoclea said. My mother wrote them down. He took out a paper and read the words:

By Air and Fire,
Water and Earth
This child shall follow the
Path of his birth,
A fire burns in him,
A fire so bright,
That all will see it
On a fateful night
when our paths will cross
and my words will be spoken
and the sound and the light
will continue, unbroken.

His hands were shaking, and the members of his troupe came forward and hugged him. Karma gave him her handkerchief. The crowd was applauding, and there was a standing ovation. Karma spoke for them all...

"I thank all of you for your appreciation of our performance. I think that it is time that we all move on to the Sphinx. I'm sure that we all want to hear Theoclea's speech. I thank you one and all."

Theoclea stared at the sky, sitting on the edge of the platform, in front of The Sphinx, with Morain, Panelle and Pythagoras behind her. The sky was clear and full of stars, and the full moon could be seen. She had seen a flock of crows, flying across the moon, and she considered them to be among the most intelligent creatures on the earth. Not many shared her belief, but she had observed them and knew that *'they listened, and watched, and thought about things'*. She saw the cloud that was formed, that rose above the Pyramid. Then, she saw the burning torches that sailed over the top of the Pyramid under the cloud. "My 'Sign of the Delphic Oracle," she said as she smiled gratefully. "It's 'Skyfire' and his troupe."

She turned to the others-

"After that display- this speech had better be good!"

She took out the Rose Medallion from a pouch, placed it around her neck, and stared at the face of Inanna for a minute. Then she turned it over and stared at the blank side. Words appeared-the lyrics to a song:

"There'll be a change in the weather and a change in the sea, but after all, there'll be a change in me. My walk will be different, my talk and my name. Nothing about me is going to be the same." She thought about the words, and a smile appeared on her face. *'Yes, this speech had better be good,' she thought.* She placed the Rose Medallion back in the pouch.

Morain and Panelle then descended from the platform, and went over to a tent to meditate. There was another tent, reserved for Theoclea, and she descended from the platform and entered it. Pythagoras saw Eimon approaching and indicated to her that all was well, and showed her the chair that had been reserved for her on the front row. There were also chairs for the children and Vorios, and they would be arriving shortly.

Finally, back at the Great Pyramid, the crowd was urged to move on, joined by all of the entertainers. They gathered around the Paws of the Sphinx. They saw that a platform had been built between the paws, with a stairway that led up to it. They all saw the tents near the platform. The Heralds urged to crowd to remain respectfully silent. Everything that the Heralds said was amplified by their magic. The ten screens were set up so that everyone could see and hear. Then, Panelle and Morain emerged from their tent, walked up the stairway and stood on the platform. Morain was dressed in her finest black robe. Panelle, of course wore a fine gold colored robe specially made for the occasion. Panelle had inspected the area in the days preceding the speech and had put up Wards and Spells. They were all in place. Morain sent out waves of empathy to the huge crowd. The crowd remained respectfully quiet. Then,

Theoclea emerged from her tent- she walked slowly up the stairway, and for a moment she imagined that in the distance she saw the Gate of Eleusis with its Crystal Lanterns to the right of the huge crowd. She stopped and nodded at the imagined Gate, then proceeded up the stairs, and confidently took her place between Panelle and Morain.

Chapter Fifteen... The Speech

Theoclea stood between the paws of the Sphinx, dressed in the red, black and gold of her station. To the right of her, Panelle scanned the crowd, a worried look on her face. The crowd was huge, estimates range from one hundred thousand to half a million people, but the wards and spells were in place-she felt sure of that. To the left of Theoclea, Morain watched the crowd, using all of her powers of empathy. The size of the crowd and the immense size and age of the statue behind them were having a profound effect on her.

The paws of the Sphinx were each the size of one of the boats that had been used for Theoclea and the members of her entourage to make the journey. In all, sixteen of the boats were used. It wasn't just the people and the things that they needed on a daily basis-there were all kinds of magical items as well, and more. The Heralds, for instance, had brought with them special crystal lantern powered devices that instantly translated Theoclea's remarks into other languages, and amplified her words.

Many people in the crowd had read her book 'Whispers'-for it had been translated into a language that most Egyptians of the higher classes were familiar with. It had been also been translated into the 'demotic' language of the middle and lower class Egyptians, as well as into many other languages. Some Egyptians, especially those of the middle, or lower classes had simply had the book read to them. They were all equally knowledgeable about the great speech that she had given at Eleusis, and they knew that the speech began with Theoclea's magical chant of childhood, 'It's starting' repeated three times. It was a simple chant that indicated to everyone that she had retained the gifts bestowed upon her as a child, a way of reminding everyone of what *they* may have lost. She also was presenting herself as a 'seer', one to be listened to. Confidently, she spoke the words, and looked at the crystal in front of her, on a stand.

"It's starting!" Everyone heard the words in Egyptian or other languages simultaneously as she spoke them. There was a response-it was something that they had to do-the crowd responded immediately- they repeated her words back to her-in whatever language they were

144

familiar with. It was as if all the languages of humanity had pondered a single thought for a moment. "It's Starting!" she said again- and the response was louder- there were many languages-so many-the crowd included people from neighboring countries, and other parts of the known and unknown world. Through the magic of the Heralds, everyone heard her.

Nubians responded in their own language-other people who spoke a form of Hebrew responded in that language- other languages could be heard as well. Then the noise died down. Theoclea held up her pouch for all to see. The crowd was silent. She took out the Red Key and placed it around her neck- there was spontaneous applause that gathered like a huge wave and then broke with a triumphant crash. She held the pouch up and waited for the noise to die down. She brought out the Rose Medallion, the Token of Inanna. Again it was like another wave triumphantly reaching the shore.

The presence of the Medallion indicated to everyone that although she was both a Priestess of Apollo and Dionysus, she needed the balance provided by the ancient Sumerian Goddess Inanna to deliver the message that she had brought with her. The crowd again applauded spontaneously and courteously-even those who disagreed with her applauded her courage in displaying the emblems of her faith.

She held up both hands and made the sign of the 'Gate of Eleusis, and in a voice that could be heard by all- again, through the powers of the Heralds, she whispered "It's starting"- there were tears in her eyes, for she realized that this would be the last time that she would use the words in a public speech. There was a hush-many people whispered 'It's starting' That was of course, expected. It was like a sizzle on an immense cymbal. She wiped her eyes with a cloth that Morain had passed to her. She looked at the cloth as if it were a piece of the relic of an ancient shroud, a *relic* and for an instant she looked at Morain- Her eyes said much. Morain knew what she would say next-

She said, for all to hear- "It all depends on *you, all* of you. *You are the Key*-That's what I said to the pilgrims at Eleusis! *You are the key.*"

There was silence, and then a resounding round of applause...she had begun with the words, magic and thoughts of the Eleusis speech-they all knew her book, and were privileged to hear her say the words. Then the applause died down. Was she going to give the Eleusis speech again?

146

"I sense that you're all familiar with the Eleusis speech. You've read it, or someone has read it to you, or perhaps someone has quoted from it. I'm going to give you some other things to consider." She smiled, returned the cloth to Morain, and confidently returned to her normal voice.

"I'll start by giving you eight upward steps, through which you can obtain blessedness, respect, honor, magic, wonder, and a hint of the divine in your lives. I hope that you find beauty and inspiration in my words, for I have a very personal...attitude when it comes to these things."

"First, you should be free to do *your work* in this life, as long as you do not harm anyone. Yes, I know what you're thinking-she can say that, she's The Oracle, it's easy for *her* to say. Does this mean that we all must be vegetarians? Some farmers use potions to kill insects that ruin their crops. You might be thinking- It's easy for her to say that we must not kill those insects'-once again-she's The Oracle."

"I only ask that you *consider and understand* the consequences of what you do-*consider* what harm is done. It's your *thoughtfulness* that I ask for."

"The second thing that I wish to ask of you is-think about *why* you were born into this lifetime, this culture, this time-what are the goals of this incarnation? In the end, is anyone going to say of you *'she did it, she made it, she reached the final gate?"*

"Is the goal of this incarnation for you to be a person who is hated and feared by humanity and history?"

"Now consider this-some of you out there are teachers, and you feel the responsibility to pass on your magical, mathematical, scientific, or spiritual teachings to others. We have artists, musicians, dancers, people who entertain with fire-the list goes on and on. Pythagoras is one of those people- he has chosen to teach his mathematics and philosophy to others. He thinks, he reads, and he listens, and he is open to new ideas, no matter how fanciful they may be."

"Think about this"-she smiled and pointed at the Sphinx behind her. "The great statue behind me may be far older than you think. Perhaps the original face was somewhat different. I'm going to shock you now, by saying perhaps it was originally the face of a Goddess of ancient Nubia! Perhaps the face is the face of an Atlantean woman, one of the first to arrive here after the great catastrophe that engulphed Atlantis!" She turned, looked at the face of the Sphinx, then back at the crowd.

She smiled, laughed, and the crowd as a whole laughed with her. Morain helped with this. Theoclea had them-it was well known that her gift was the gift of choosing the right words at the right time, as well as seeing the past, present, and future in her own way. She probably had many more gifts, and everyone was at least somewhat open to her views.

"You're all laughing with me, but it might be true!" She smiled and laughed again, and turned her palms up, as if sharing a secret. She had their full attention. She had them.

She continued when the laughter died down. "I am charged with the responsibility to see that the dreams of Orpheus, the great priest, shall become a reality."

"He stopped the blood sacrifice in the Greek Temples-that was over 700 to 1000 years ago, possibly more."

"He is credited with introducing new Gods and Goddesses into the Pagan tradition of Greece. Some of this is true, and some fanciful. He is credited with writing the beautiful and haunting invocations to the

Gods and Goddesses that are spoken at the Mysteries of Eleusis. There is much more that may be truth or myth, or perhaps something in between."

"This I will say is true- He dreamed of having the Temple of Delphi represent two opposing views-the Light and the Dark-Apollo and Dionysus represented in the same Temple. He realized that a Goddess was needed to insure balance, and for some reason he chose to pass the Rose Medallion, the Token of Inannna on to the Priestess that would represent all of these views. *I am the one who has chosen to do this!*"

The crowd responded with shouts of her name-a high declaration of their esteem. She continued:

"All that I ask is that you listen. I listen more than I speak, I listen for the whispers."

"I *see*, I look for all that will increase the richness and vitality, not just of the Greek people, but all of us. We all share a common history. You may interpret my words as you will. *I ask that you just listen."*

She stared at the face of Inanna on the Rose Medallion for a minute, the crowd was very quiet...then she turned the medallion over-and said:

"The Medallion asks me to speak more, and suggests that I have four or five other things to convey to you, and so I shall-when the medallion speaks to me *I listen. I will also relate the contents of a vision that I have had, while here in Egypt.*"

"We all have choices to make at every stage of our lives. Some of the choices seem to compete with each other, and some seem to cooperate well with our paths and temperaments. It is your duty and responsibility to yourselves and others to seek harmony and balance. Reality is a web of possible outcomes and consequences. My gift is that I see the possible consequences, and can advise people...but your goddess Ma'at, for instance represents the web that is always in the background-working its' way through consequences- a web or net of consequences-you are better to seek harmony with Ma'at-always seek harmony and balance with Ma'at."

"Some of you may know of the Qabala- The Tree of Life- If you do, then stand in the point of Tiphareth. Say to yourself "*Tiphareth chose me*" Place yourself in Tiphareth- Think about what are the consequences to the greater good. What is best for me as I move through the Tree of Life. Tiphareth is where so many paths meet. The meaning in Hebrew is *beauty*, but I also see it as a meeting place for the opposites, the Light and Dark,

Apollo and Dionysus- Perhaps you see it as the light and warmth of Ra- Tiphareth has many interpretations-the lion-the phoenix-centrality-wholeness, and more."

"Next, I want to tell you of what I consider to be the many ways of using your thoughts to come to conclusions-ways of using your wits, perhaps. Are you stuck in the path of reducing everything to its simplest form so that you can analyze the situation? I certainly am not that way, but perhaps Pythagoras is." She smiled and looked across to Pythagoras-seated on the front row. "Did he learn to think that way while he spent eleven years studying to be a Priest in your land?"

There was some laughter, and Pythagoras smiled. The children Alcena and Abderus were on either side of him their beaming faces showed the pride that they had in their mother and father. All of them were aware that she was giving perhaps the greatest speech of a lifetime of speaking, writing, and listening.

" I'll tell you a secret-she reached her right hand out as if to beckon to Pythagoras-"Pythagoras wrote some lovely poetry while he was studying to be a Priest-and he's read it to me" She smiled at him and the children once more. "My thinking seems to be more creative-aesthetic- and yes, of course intuitive. That's because of my gifts, and the visions and dreams that accompany me. Oh I know what you're thinking now- Why is Theoclea being so serious? I'll tell you why-because all of this thinking must be balanced by your knowledge of the Earth. I know that earlier in your history there was a forty year famine that almost destroyed your great civilization. After that you found ways to prepare for the unexpected surprises that the Earth itself can throw your way. The Nile is your heart, but that has not always been so. You are prepared now for the unforeseen. The Atlanteans were not so fortunate. Use your Heart, Imagination, Intelligence, Courage, and above all have Spiritual Hope. Believe in those who have 'got your back'."

"Theoclea asks you-"Who's got your back? Unfamiliar words! Those words came to me from the far future on the Rose Medallion. 'Who's got your back?' The Gods, The Goddesses, The Muses, a God, A Goddess? You must believe-it is your belief that strengthens the existence of the Spirits on the other planes. Your thoughts become and strengthen their forms. Believe and trust in them-they are not infallible-but magic will be your reward. A song to a musician, a poem to a poet- a formula to a mathematician, the list of magic goes on and on."

"I have been asked this question many times-'Theoclea, is there anything that you consider to be simply *wrong? My answer is a resounding yes!* I consider all acts that interfere with the free will or evolutionary process of an individual, or population of individuals to be *wrong.* Do not ask for Magic spells that will force a person to bend to your will. The Temple of Delphi was attacked a year ago, by descendants of Atlantis-The Sons of Belial, led by an evil man named Davros."

"Davros was killed by a magical act that involved the bonding of four women, Bella, the dancer, myself, and two of my dearest childhood friends, Anka, the queen of Hydros, and Troyana, The Sybil. I was able to foresee the scenario-and saw that the consequence of his acts would be his death. I saw that before I even met him. He had me, bound and drugged, in a room where he desecrated the altar of Gaia! The bonding of the women occurred before I met him, but I must admit, that a part of me knew that our bonding was necessary for the scenario to play its way out. I was in harmony with your Goddess Ma'at, and you might say that she spoke to me about what would happen."

"It was Davros' actions that created the course that led to his death. Each man in Davros' army is now followed by a stone that rests in his yard, or on his boat or wherever he may be. If any one of them would commit a wrongful act against another, the stone will kill them. They do not know which stone it is. Does that mean that they can never defend themselves, when another moves against them? *No, but they must always think of the consequences.*"

"*Perhaps those stones are the stones of peace...and that is another matter completely-do instruments of destruction lead to Peace? It is not within the scope of my speech to you tonight to speak of this. I will move on.*"

"Two more points that I want you to consider, and then, I will relate to you a vision. You are all bearers of the Divine spark of the Great Ones. Look for the presence of the divine in all of the beings that we interact with in our lives, using higher love as our goal. I often look at the birds, and wonder about them. I have heard that the crow is among the most intelligent of birds. Do you know that a crow can use tools and can recognize one human face from another? Do not make assumptions-all beings on this planet have the Divine Spark within them."

"The last point that I want to impart to you is simply this-We should ever be mindful that the Earth is our mother and honor that sacred relationship."

"I will conclude my speech by telling you of a vision that I had last night. It is not the first vision that I have had in the tent. It appeared in a dream I had as I was asleep. I have never in all my life shared a vision with such a large crowd-this will probably be the first and last time that I shall do this."

"In my dream, or vision, I saw a very large tent, similar to a tent that I visited on the continent of Atlantis almost 9000 years ago. Now it can be told- Pythagoras, Vorios, Panelle, Morain and I visited Atlantis in a vision. I saw the destruction of Atlantis, and many other things happened as well. At that time we all decided not to tell the story, agreeing that no one would believe it. We all experienced a group vision of some kind that was very real physically. We were all in a tent made up of triangular shaped canvas structures laced together with leather poles tried at the top."

"In Egypt last night I saw the tent again, but it was much bigger, I was alone, and it was night. Imagine that the tent was over there on that plain." She pointed to a level area beyond the Pyramids and the Sphinx. Many heads turned to where Theoclea was pointing. "The tent in my dream the other night was all lit up by crystal lanterns, they hung from all of the poles. It was decorated on the outside with symbols from many religions of the past and the present, as well as strange symbols from future religions, among them was the Pentacle with the four Roses, a sign that I mention in the 'Whispers' book. Here and there the symbol of the Red Key was repeated on the canvas, as well as the Gold Key and the Black key. On the door to the tent was a large Red Key, but above the door there was a Silver Key, and below the Key there were words in a language that I seemed to know in the dream-the words said 'Know ye the Truth of the Moment, and Enter of your own Free Will!'"

"I opened the flap, and entered the tent. There was a circular table, and there were six men, and six women seated around the table, the men on one side, and the women on the other side. Between them there was one empty chair. The table was set for a feast. When they saw me, they stood up and approached me one by one. I recognized some of them, I had seen their faces on the Rose Medallion. There were tears in their eyes, and they used words from their languages that I seemed to know-all of the words meant 'welcome'-then –they pointed to a chair, a thirteenth chair at the far end of the circle, and one of them guided me over to the chair."

"They all sat down, but not in their original places, the men and the women were interspersed."

Tears appeared once again in Theoclea's eyes, and she motioned to Morain for the cloth. Pythagoras sat on the front row. He sat forward, rapt in attention. She had not mentioned this dream to him. The children sat forward as well. They had been told stories by their mother, but this one was different. Theoclea wiped her eyes, and gave the cloth back to Morain, who glanced at Panelle. Panelle nodded to Morain, and glanced up at the stars, as if to say "The Wards and Spells are all in place, all is well."

Theoclea continued-

"The tent was somewhat dark-there were candles, but my eyes have begun to have a blindness in the dark, I suppose it comes with age. I was led to the open seat, and saw that there was no candle in front of me. Then one man from across the room came toward me with a golden candle. There was a stand in front of me that was large enough to accommodate perhaps half a dozen candles, and he placed the golden candle on the stand, saying-

"No one lights a lamp and puts it in a place where it will be hidden, or under a bowl. Instead he puts it on its stand, so that those who come in may see the light."

He smiled at me and returned to his seat.

Next, a woman approached me. She held a black candle, placed it before me on the stand, and said,

"I bring you words from the Zohar- The golden light of a candle flame sits upon the throne of its' dark light that clings to the wick."

She then returned to her seat.

A man then stood up and approached me with a red candle, placing it on the stand, he said,

"Across planes of consciousness we have to live with the paradox that opposite things can simultaneously be true." He then returned to his seat.

I looked in front of me and I saw food, but I can't remember what I ate in the vision. It was a simple meal, I can tell you that. I remember that there was wine. You all know that I enjoy a glass of wine. After all, I am a Priestess of Dionysus as well as Apollo. The wine and the light were in front of me. Then a woman stood up and approached me.

She stood beside me, and said,

"The first one to to hold the seat of Prophecy was Gaia-the Earth. The earth has light and dark aspects. It is our home, and we rejoice when the sunlight touches us. The dark aspect of the earth is that she can be indiscriminate in her destructiveness."

"The second to hold the seat of Prophecy was Themis-Tradition. You are part of a great tradition, Theoclea, and have shared your wisdom with others. You will be remembered for this."

Then she said-

"I am the third to hold the Seat of Prophecy-Phoebe-'The Bright and Shining One', and I give you this gift."

Theoclea paused...looked down, and then out at the immense crowd.

"She gave me a Rose. Then my vision ended."

She closed her eyes, took a big breath, and then smiled at the crowd. Then, her expression became serious, and for about three seconds that seemed to be an eternity, she looked at Morvan, her unblinking eyes revealed that the moment had come. Morvan, who stood at the end of the first row, returned her gaze, a serious expression on his face. Pythagoras quickly glanced from one to another. He sat forward in his seat.

"I leave you with a mystery to ponder-the words of a song of the future appeared to me on the Rose Medallion tonight. As usual, my words mingled with the words that I saw-you all know that words have a fascination for me, for the right words at the right time are always expected of me. People are always asking me these questions..."

"Theoclea, can you give us a prophecy of the future? Perhaps you can give us some inspiring words about transformation, or reincarnation."

"I believe that the words of this song address these issues." She smiled mischievously at Morain and Panelle. "The name of the song is-'There'll be some changes made'."

Pythagoras held his breath *'What...?'* he thought.

"There'll be a change in the weather
and a change in the sea-
But most of all there'll be a change in me"

She paused and once more glanced at Morvan for a moment.

"My walk will be different
My talk and my name
Nothing about me is going to be the same."

She paused once again, and looked out at the crowd- Her eyes met The Scribe's...He smiled and saw where she was going...

"I'm going to learn some words of magic,
And if that's not enough,
I'll be a Healer
I can do that kind of stuff!"

She paused again and looked at Morain and Panelle-They were both beaming-they had broad smiles on their faces-she looked at her children-they were proud of their mother, and it showed in their faces as well.

"You think nobody will like you when you're old and gray?"

She took a lock of her hair that had some gray in it-shook it so that everyone could see it- then looked at Eimon – her red hair- and smiled.

She held up her right arm and made a fist with her hand.

"There'll be some changes made today!"

She turned to both Morain and Panelle...they continued to smile broadly she held hands with them, and then all three raised their hands and she said, for all to hear-

"There'll be some changes made!"

162

"Thank you one and all for listening to me. I thank my Guardian Panelle and my Counselor Morain. I am the Pythia, the Pythian Priestess, the Dragon Priestess of the Earth, I am a Priestess of Apollo, as well as a Priestess of Dionysus. I am the Oracle of the glorious Temple of Delphi. I wear the Rose Medallion and the Red Key
I am also a follower of Inanna,
her symbol was-The Rose"
All three lowered their hands and bowed to the audience.

There was overwhelming applause, and a standing ovation. Eimon, Miriam, and Priori, sat with the children and Pyhagoras, on the first row, and they joined the standing ovation. Once more, Theoclea's eyes filled with tears, and she motioned to Morain for the cloth again. She wiped the tears from her eyes., and noted that Morain had a look of concern on her face. She turned to Panelle who was gazing at the sky.

Suddenly the scene froze. It was, as always, as if .... Theoclea looked around slowly, and saw Morain-Morain was frozen in a look of concern. Theoclea turned to Panelle, who was still looking up at the sky. Not a sound was heard.

163

There were the amorphous lights in the sky once again. Suddenly the scene whirled around her and changed. The three of them were in a vast cathedral. Light and color came back and Theoclea saw stained glass windows. Then, Theoclea saw a woman, a Priestess of the far future. She was holding the cloth that Theoclea had just used to wipe her tears. The woman was saying something:

"We only bring this out for a few days during the year. It is kept in the relics room in a glass case that is temperature-controlled. The cloth was on a silk cushion, and the Priestess moved amongst a crowd of what seemed to be tourists. "It is the cloth that Theoclea used to wipe away her tears as she ended her speech to a vast crowd on a platform between the paws of The Sphinx. She used it at other times as well during the speech. It is the cloth that Morain held for her."

Theoclea looked about…There seemed to be a crowd of tourists. One of the tourists said "Has this cloth ever been carbon-dated?" The Priestess looked at him, and then at the cloth. *There is no need to carbon-date the cloth-It is the cloth that Theoclea used to wipe away her tears!*"

Theoclea turned her head quickly and saw that the large stained glass window was becoming transparent- and in the distance she could see the Sphinx and the

Pyramids. The Cathedral was in Egypt! Suddenly she turned back to look at the Priestess, and noticed that there was a Priest standing next to her, and he held something in his hands-it was The Book. He had a look of grave concern on his face and glanced in Theoclea's direction. Suddenly, she collapsed. A point of light returned and grew, and she saw familiar faces and heard familiar voices around her. Pythagoras and the children rushed up on the stage when they saw her collapse-Eimon, Miriam and Priori were already there. Morain and Panelle of course held her up. She opened her eyes and was stunned. Then a smile slowly grew on her face. She looked down and there was the cloth in her hands. She wiped her eyes and then proceeded to hug everyone. Eimon came over, and looked at Theoclea and then at the cloth. She hugged Eimon, and Eimon said "I know, this has all been- a bit much for you." Eimon was in tears. "The speech was wonderful-so beautiful. I was very moved by your words"

Theoclea tilted her head and said to Eimon "Here use this cloth to wipe away your tears." Eimon did so, and returned the cloth to Theoclea. Pythagoras and the children hugged her and asked how she felt. She said: "I feel blessed, very blessed, I have almost everything that..." She then looked at the cloth, and turned

165

to Morain. "Morain, please keep this cloth as a remembrance of this day."

Pythagoras stared at her, she turned back to him and returned his gaze. "The words to the song..." he started to say. Theoclea cut him off. "I have everything, but there are one or two more things that I must do... for Orpheus" She smiled and kissed him Then they all turned and waved at the crowd-a crowd that was still standing, and still applauding.

Only one person was not applauding, he stood to the side, his arms folded. 'She knows, *she knows!* He must have told her!-he thought.' Then he changed his mind, and shook his head. 'No, he didn't have to tell her, *she knows, she sees, she hears-all'-* Morvan kept his arms folded, shaking his head in disbelief.

Chapter Sixteen... They enter the Giza Pyramid

The children were well aware of the difficulty of what they all were about to do. Vorios and Pythagoras had discussed the tools that would be needed, and what would have to be done. It was early morning, and they were dressed properly and prepared.

"This mystery-about the lost book-it's just the kind of a mystery that always finds me," Alcena said.

"What do you mean by that?" Abderus replied.

"Well, it's just that ever since I had that vision while Davros held a knife to my throat, I've wondered about what my life's work would be," said Alcena. "I've decided to be a kind of a-what was that word-detective, and solve mysteries!"

"...and where does that leave me? I've had to protect you lots of times. Remember that time when you wandered away from the other orphans, and no one could hardly find you? Who was it that figured out that you'd be hiding behind one of the stones in the big half circle of stones! I'd say that it's not Mystery, but trouble that always finds you, Alcena!"

Alcena simply ignored him and gathered her tools together, a crystal lantern, a whisk broom, magnifying glass, various sized hammers and chisels, and bags to hold anything that might be found. Abderus was equally well prepared.

Pythagoras, Vorios, Alcena and Abderus met at the planned meeting place, and headed for the Great Pyramid of Giza. They had The Scribe's instructions with them.

They walked around the Pyramid, and found the base of the white line, then carefully measured the distance until they were standing in front of the stones that the Scribe had indicated. Pythagoras had his wand and his staff, and was sure that they were capable of lifting or pulling stone blocks that weighed many tons.

Suddenly, Vorios took out a crystal wand and pointed it at the first stone. There was a hum as a steady beam of light from Vorios' wand hit the stone. The light started to change colors, until it matched the frequency of the stone, then, the stone came forward slowly, with an audible screech, as if pulled magnetically by the beam of the crystal wand. When it finally came out completely, Vorios moved it forward, and gently placed it on the ground.

"Vorios, you never told me that you had a crystal wand!" Pythagoras said.

"It is over 10,000 years old, and I have not used it recently. I've had it since the time of my youth on Atlantis. I hope that it still has enough power to do the work required of it today."

The children both looked with wide eyes at each other.

"Atlantis-a crystal wand!" They both said at the same time.

Vorios tried the wand on the other two stones-the wand worked-the other two stones were lifted out and suspended in the air, and then gently lowered to the ground. Pythagoras and Vorios climbed up on the stone blocks and tried to enter the opening, but the way was blocked by debris.

"Here's where we come in," Alcena said. "Come on Abderus, we're small enough to clear the way."

The children turned their crystal lanterns on, and started to crawl in. They passed the shards and fragments of stone out to Vorios and Pythagoras. Finally, there was an opening big enough for all to enter. They all crawled in about ten feet, and found themselves in the internal ramp that The Scribe had spoken of. They then moved to the right, slowly inspecting all of the stones on the left wall, until they came to the stone that bore The Scribe's symbol-three interlocking crystals.

Vorios told the others to stand back. He used the crystal wand on the stone, and it worked, slowly the stone screeched forward. Suddenly, the air in the ramp seemed to be teeming with dark bat-like shapes.

"They're not bats, they're Tomb Wraiths, everyone down," shouted Vorios.

He looked at his crystal wand, and turned it on, but it was losing power. 'One more time, just one more time', he thought. He turned it on high and swirled it round and round in the air. One by one the Tomb Wraiths disappeared in puffs of smoke until they were all gone. The wand had used up a great deal of power.

"Now let's try it on the stone, and get the book."

The wand was aimed at the stone-the beam was weak and changed into all of the colors of the spectrum once again, until the frequency of the stone was found. Inch by inch ever so slowly, the stone moved and creaked forward until it fell out from the wall, and at that instant Vorios' wand lost all of its' power. With all of their crystal lanterns on they could clearly see that indeed the book was there, behind the stone. Vorios reached for the book, held it gently in his hands, and removed it, when all of a sudden, they heard a voice-

"Not so fast, you'll now have to deal with us!"

Vorios whirled to his right and left. Coming at them from opposite sides of the ramp were-Muhajihadeem!

Chapter Seventeen... The Muhajihadeem and The Projector

"Muhajihadeem!" Vorios shouted at the others, "stand still." The Muhajihadeem approached slowly. They were dressed in black hooded robes and their faces could not be seen. Each one carried a razor sharp scimitar.

"You didn't think that it would be easy, to just come in here and leave with that priceless book did you?" one of them said.

The other one laughed, and said,

"He will pay us a great deal for that book, now just hand it over to me." They approached cautiously, then the first one walked up the wall of the ramp, and stood upside down on the ceiling.

"You see, we can appear anywhere, walk up walls, even stand on the ceiling."

173

"We control forces that you are not aware of." The other one walked up the wall, and stood upside down on the ceiling as well.

"We can even exchange scimitars," both of them said at the same time. Each one dropped his scimitar and the blades floated along the ceiling, passed each other, and wound up in the other one's hands. In an instant they were both once again standing on the floor.

"We can appear anywhere-for instance..."

Suddenly one of them stood behind Alcena, his blade almost touching her throat. She was held in the grip of some force. The other one appeared as well, holding his scimitar to Abderus' throat.

"Now Vorios, Pythagoras, be reasonable, all you have to do is give us the book, and the children will be unharmed."

Alcena took a deep breath, and instantly the scene was frozen, as if a frame of black and white film was stuck in in an old projector. She saw that everyone, including the Muhajihadeem was frozen in the moment. In a flash, she saw three moving lights that got brighter and brighter, until three women could be seen. There was one dressed in a gold robe with blonde hair, holding out a crystal wand. The symbol of the three interlocking crystals that they had seen on the stone was on the back of her robe. Another woman was dressed in a black robe, with the same symbol on the back, and had black hair. She executed a complex dance step and then made a complicated hand gesture. The third figure was the most commanding of the three-she had red hair and looked like an older version of Eimon. She wore a robe of red, gold and black, and had a crown of three crystals on her head.

She turned to the blonde woman and shouted, "Sonja!" Sonja aimed and fired her crystal wand at the first Muhajihadeem, and then whirled and fired it again at the other one. The red-haired woman then said "Aura! Send the calm and empathy." Aura made a quick dance move, and gestured with her hands. The scene was still frozen, but Alcena saw all of it. The red-haired woman with the crown then approached the book that was in Vorios' hands. She stared at it, put her hands together and made the 'Sign of the gate of Eleusis'. She looked at Vorios, as if trying to remember something. The three women then disappeared, and all color, light and motion came back.

Vorios was standing there with the book, and the Muhajihadeem were gone.

"What happened?" Abderus said, shaking his head. He felt a strange sense of calm.

"I saw it all, I had a vision of it!" Alcena said. She related the vision to them.

"We were saved by the three women from Atlantis, Sonja, Aura, and the Queen, Axcelotl, my mother... They are now..."

"The Spirits of Eternal Vigilance," Vorios said. He paused for a moment, and then said-"We've got the book, let's get out of here before anything else happens!"

"Yes," Pythagoras said, "there may be more Muhajihadeem!"

"Wait," said Abderus, "look ahead, there is a light flickering on the wall at the end of the ramp."

"Yes," Alcena said. "We can't leave, we must see what it is! It could be another part of the mystery here!"

"All right," Pythagors said. They all carefully approached the source of the flickering light. They reached the end of the ramp, and saw something lying on the ground. It was obviously incredibly old-it seemed to be a black box with a crystal lantern on the inside. There was a roll of transparent thin tape-like material in front of the box on a spool of some kind, and a similar spool below it. In between there was a metal tube that contained some kind of magnifying material. The lantern was flickering on and off, as if it was dying. They looked at the image that was projected on the wall.

"That's the Temple in the Sand of Atlantis, as it was over 9000 years ago," Pythagoras said. 'Do you see the steps leading up to the Temple?" He looked at Vorios, and said, "We were all there, Vorios, what is this device?" Vorios looked at Pythagoras, and then at the object. "It is an ancient projector, from Atlantis, and it seems to be stuck on one frame of the 'film' as we called it. There's a motor here, powered by a Crystal Lantern. Vorios hesitated before saying more- "These 'projectors' were mainly used by women of the Temple who would see the images, and hear the music, and go into trance in the way that Theoclea does when she inhales the Dragon's breath. They were Oracles!"

"Wow", Alcena and Abderus said at practically the same time. Vorios looked at Pythagoras and said, "I think that we should keep this a secret-it's too fragile to take with us-let's ponder this-all of us-we have The Book, and it may give us more answers. We can always come back and look at the 'projector' again."

"No one must tell Theoclea, or any of the others-this must remain a secret between the four of us, until the time comes to reveal it." He made them all swear an oath-The children continued to stare at the object.

Pythagoras said, "There's no way to keep this a secret from Theoclea, she seems to see and know almost everything that happens-but we can try."

Then, Alcena said "I don't have to look for mysteries, they find me," she said with a satisfied grin. Abderus replied-"Well...I still think that you're always going to need my protection. You're hardly able to defend yourself, you need me for that."

She shrugged, then they walked back along the ramp. Pythagoras saw the stone with the sign of the three crystals on it, and aimed his wand and staff at it. It rose, and he gently put it back in place.

Vorios looked at Pythagoras' wand and staff, smiled, and said,

"If I knew that you could do that, I wouldn't have used my wand!"

They all laughed. Vorios carried the book, they left the ramp and crawled outside. They walked back to the tents after Pythagoras used his wand and his staff to return all of the stones back to their original places. The children had never seen Pythagoras use his wand or staff. They both looked at each other and grinned. Inside the Great Pyramid, the Crystal Lamp on the 'projector' stopped flickering, and went out, never to shine its' light again. The 'projector' had been powered by the Crystal Lamp, and, having achieved its' final purpose-it simply-disappeared!

Chapter Eighteen... Theoclea knows, and sees The Book

Pythagoras showed her the book the next day. They went over it page by page, admiring the drawings, and puzzling over the text. Pythagoras' enthusiasm was greater than Theoclea's, but she tried to hide her skepticism, for she knew what this 'find' meant to him.

"Is there something more, Pythagoras?" she said quietly.

"No, Theoclea, there were scenes on the walls-you know-the picture writing-I've tried to remember what they looked like-He looked at her with a furtive glance-"Well, we have the book!"

"I know," said Theoclea, "and you saw the 'projector'."

He put his hand on his forehead-closed his eyes and then opened them.

"I should know by now that I can't keep secrets from you. Then he frowned "Did...someone tell you about it?"

"No, I *simply knew, Pythagoras.* I saw the projector in a vision-and my visions have always started with the feeling-as if it were there. It is more than a mere machine. Several of them were used by women who were specially trained to work with them and their images, as well as sounds. There were Oracles on Atlantis, Pythagoras. Axcelotl, the Queen was not one of them, but there were other women in other rooms in the Temple in the Sand."

She told him more, and then he gave her the book.

"If you don't mind, Pythagoras, I'd like to be alone with this book, and study its' pages." Pythagoras smiled, sighed, and said,

"Yes, I understand. The Scribe was right, you are a treasure, and I should never let you go!" He kissed her and left the tent, to let her ponder The Book.

He somehow had an awareness, that the Goddess Ma'at was involved in all of this, and if so, it was Theoclea, of all people, who would be aware of this, and know how to deal with it.

She sat down with the book, and pondered its' pages one by one, and with each page a growing sense of uneasiness settled in.

She didn't like what she saw.

Chapter Nineteen... The Star Children in trouble

Alcena and Abderus had decided to go alone to a site that the other children told them about, a site at which the other children had found shards of ancient pottery, and coins. They had their small whisk brooms, chisels, hammers, and magnifying glasses. They both wore hats to protect them from the sun, and had canteens filled with water, sugar, and various herbs that Theoclea had put in the water. Alcena had decided that they would sneak out, and not have Morain and Panelle go with them.

"After all, this is a mystery, and mystery surrounds us here."

"But what if there's trouble, and I can't hardly protect you-don't you think that we should tell Morain and Panelle about this?" Abderus replied.

"It wouldn't be a mystery if we let Morain and Panelle in on it! Quickly, let's go before they find out that we've gone somewhere!"

They walked outside of the tent, and Alcena pointed in a certain direction-"Let's go this way," she said.

"But if we go that way, we'll reach the edge of the fields, the desert is in that direction!"

'I know that," Alcena said. "That's where the other kids told us to go-do you have your bag with you? We're gonna find some treasure!"

"I forgot my bag," he said. "Wait a moment, it's in the tent."

"Why must I always remind you of everything, Abderus. Where would you be without me?"

"Sleeping in the tent right now," Abderus replied. "I'll be right back."

He came back shortly-"Okay, I'm ready, let's go. They walked in the direction that Alcena had indicated, and in due time, they came to the edge of a fertile savannah, along the banks of the Nile.

"I think that we should continue in the same direction," Alcena said.

"But you're taking us out into the desert, and we were told not to go there," Abderus cautioned.

"Do you see that small Pyramid directly ahead of us, Abderus? That's where the other kids told us to go! That's where they dug up the coins and pottery." Alcena walked ahead about ten steps into the desert.

"Don't be afraid, Abderus, it's all right, come on, it's a mystery." He started to walk toward her. Neither of them noticed that 10 feet to the right of him was crystal in the shape of a Pentagon, and ten feet to the left of him, there was a Tetrahedron-shaped Crystal. When he caught up to her, he looked ahead, and saw it. Directly ahead of them, about ten feet away, was a crystal in the shape of an Obelisk.

"Look, Abderus...a crystal-we've already found something!" She started to walk toward it, but Abderus saw the crystal and immediately looked back to his left and right.

"No, Alcena, it's a trap-Pythagoras warned me about this!"

It was too late. Suddenly they were standing in a narrow street of a great city. In the distance, they could see the Pyramids, the Giza Plateau, and the Sphinx, about a half mile away, at the end of the street. Ahead of them was a bustling Metropolis with skyscrapers. People were walking by, seemingly not noticing them.

"I think that we should go that way-back toward the Sphinx and the Pyramids,"Abderus said.

Alcena looked about in puzzled wonder.

"Where are we, and when are we? It's a mystery! We're in a real mystery, and we're detectives-we have to figure this out!"

"It's no mystery to me," Abderus said, "we're in Cairo, and it's way in the future."

He turned toward the end of the street, the Pyramids and the Sphinx. "They should be ten miles away!" Abderus said.

Suddenly someone completely dressed in black, holding a large sharp scimitar appeared on the street. His black hooded robe did not show his face, and he was walking slowly and menacingly toward them.

"He's hardly a mystery to me, either! He's a Muhajihadeem-an assassin! Run, Alcena, run."

Chapter Twenty...The Muhajihadeem-Again

They ran down the street, and saw a metal ladder attached to the side of a building. The ladder led to a metal platform with another ladder, that led to another platform. Something that people of the future would call a 'Fire Escape'. The ladders and platforms went all the way up the side of the building. The children climbed up to the first platform, then looked at the Muhajihadeem, as he watched them from below. Then they climbed another ladder to a higher level. People were coming and going on the street, but didn't seem to notice what was happening.

They looked down at the Muhajihadeem. He stood there with his hood on, his eyes suddenly shining, and said to them,

"This is a piece of cake-He will be pleased." Suddenly, he simply walked up the wall of the side of the building, to the platform above them, and stood looking down at them. Abderus looked to the right of the Muhajihadeem, and there was a sign-a red heart flashing on and off. The Muhajihadeem took his scimitar and drove it into the heart shaped sign. Sparks flashed all around and sizzled from the sign, he held onto the hilt, then he withdrew the scimitar, and laughed at them. "Nothing can kill me!" he said. Alcena was visibly shaken.

"I don't like this mystery, Abderus," she said.

"Take heart, Alcena, this must play out, it's hardly over!" he said.

The Muhajihaddim laughed at them. "This is the easiest assignment that he has given me!" He brandished his scimitar.

Suddenly, someone appeared on the platform above him. It was the dancer, Bella, of the Bella-Festa Dance Troupe. She was dressed in black and was holding her own battle-ready scimitar. She whispered something to it. Then she said, "Not so fast Muhajihadeem. I have sworn to protect these children. Don't you think that I'm a worthy adversary?"

He looked up at her. "Hah, a woman with a scimitar!" he walked up the wall, to her platform, and faced her.

"He has given me much tougher assignments in different places at different times." He swung his scimitar, but with a quick dance move, Bella avoided his blade.

"Ah," he was perplexed. "You are very agile, you are obviously a dancer." He swung his scimitar again, and again, she executed quick dance moves, and avoided his blade. It was her turn now. She smiled at him and whispered something to her sword. "Who is it that you work for Muhajihadeem?" she asked.

"That's none of your business," he proudly said.

"Well, I guess that they can make do with one less assassin." He was enraged at that remark, and swung his sword again, hitting her sword, and seemingly knocking it out of her hands. It fell over the platform. He held his blade and then said, "and now for the finish." She smiled at him.

"Yes, the finish!" she said, as her sword whirled around in the air, made a quick circle, decapitated him, and then returned to her hands. He disappeared.

She looked down at the children, and indicated the way to the desert-"Run, children, run-there will be more of him, I am sure. Run toward the Sphinx, and the Pyramids!"

Chapter Twenty-One...The Desert and the Sphinx

They headed back to the Giza plateau and the Sphinx. When they got there, they stood between the paws of the Sphinx. The paws were easily each the size of a twentieth century bus. I know, dear reader, for I have been there. Anyway, that's where they stood.

"Did you see the way that Bella's scimitar beheaded that guy," Alcena said. "The mystery widens, there's mystery all around us! We're like detectives, here to figure out the mystery," she smiled in wonderment.

"Yes, Alcena, and there's desert all around us," he looked over and the fertile savannah was nowhere to be seen. Also the scene was changing as they stood there. The city was gone. He turned around and looked at the Sphinx, The paws were disappearing, and the face was changing. The body was disappearing as well, they heard water, and he turned around. The Nile was flowing in front of the Sphinx!- and it was starting to rain."

"Where and when are we?" Alcena said.

Suddenly, the figure of Anka appeared. She was covered all over in henna tattoos, made of the magical henna that the people of Hydros used when they left the Island. When on the island, they all walked about in the nude. She quickly surveyed the scene, and took her bow and arrow, and shot it in the direction of a spot along the Nile. The arrow, magically became a tent. She said, "Quick, children, into the tent." They all ran over and entered the tent. The inside was dry, and there were cushions for them to sit on.

"I am sworn to Theoclea to protect you always. Bella, Troyana, and even Vorios are sworn to this pact. Anka put away her bow and arrows and looked out of the tent, into the pouring rain.

"You are on the plain of the Nile as it existed eight thousand years before your birth-behold the face of the Sphinx." She opened the flap and the children stared at the face of the Sphinx. It was –different. Anka continued-

"Perhaps the face of a goddess of Nubia, or a Goddess of Atlantis? The Nile flowed in front of it. At that time there were huge natural boulders called 'yardangs' that were found along the Nile. Someone, an artisan or a sculptor designed it-he had a team of men build it-he knew that it would always be seen from the Nile, but by your time, the Nile will have changed its' course. "There'll be a change in the weather, and a change in the sea," as the song goes. The face will be changed to suit the rulers of the time-it may be changed to resemble them-the body of a lion will be added, by one or more of the rulers, but the body and the paws will never be proportional to the head, and that will be the clue. Eventually the rains will stop, and the statue and its' lion-like body will be in an enclosure with a Temple in front of it, and desert all around."

"Alcena, you like a mystery, the body and the paws will show signs of weathering that can only be made by rain, yes, rain-in the Nile Delta-thousands and thousands of years before you are to be born. I have told you the Ancient story, told to me by your mother, Theoclea, to be retold at the right time- Theoclea told us the story when we were children, Theoclea, Troyana and I."

"In our child-like rituals I was always Artemis, and I balked at playing the part, but I realize now that-with the bows and arrows-and the ability to disappear and re-appear because of the magical henna, that I am very much like Artemis. I was destined to be Artemis."

"Children-you must return to the city of the future for this 'Mystery' as you put it, Alcena, to reveal itself. The mystery must reach its' ultimate conclusion. You must meet 'The Antiquarian Brotherhood'." With that she disappeared. The rain had stopped. They opened the flap of the tent, and found that the tent was back in the city, right in front of a huge skyscraper, in the modern district of the city. People were coming and going, but nobody noticed them, or the tent.

Chapter Twenty-Two... The Skyscraper

They walked into the building and they were in the anteroom of an office building. There were buttons on a wall, and slots alongside them. There was a man next to them, and he pressed a button. They heard a voice say, "Oracle Corporation", and he replied, talking into a slot- 'Smith here'...the door was buzzed open and the man opened the door, and went in, with the children quickly following him.

Alcena looked about in amazement. "We are in one of those very tall buildings of the future-even taller than the Pyramid of Giza!" They watched the man as he walked over to a board that was on the side of a large door that kept opening and closing. There were five or six other doors in a row, and people were walking into cubicles. At other cubicles, the doors opened and people walked out. They walked over to the board that the man was looking at. He saw 'Oracle Corporation' and pointed to a number beside the name: 600-616. Then he stood in front of the door and waited. Alcena looked at the board and saw 'Antiquarian Brotherhood' then the number 1212 right next to it. Suddenly, the doors opened and people rushed out. When most of them were out the man 'Smith' walked into the cubicle. They followed him. Nobody else walked into the cubicle. When they were in, the man pressed a button with a 6 on it.

Alcena went over and quickly pressed the 12 button. The man didn't even seem to notice them. There was a low hum and a feeling of vibration. They seemed to feel slightly heavier as well, and their ears popped. "Alcena," Abderus started to say. She stopped him and put a finger in front of her face, and pointed to the man. The man seemed not to have heard anything. Suddenly they noticed that the vibration that they had felt in the room seemed to stop. The doors opened and the man stepped out. They looked out and instead of a large lobby room, there was a hallway and doors, then the doors started to close, and they pulled their heads in. The hum and the feeling of slight heaviness returned. Their ears started to pop again.

"This is a room that is going up through the building. When the doors open, we are on a different level, Alcena said.

"It doesn't take a detective to figure that out," Abderus replied, "Now what are we going to do about it?"

The humming then stopped and the doors opened. There was a door in front of them in a hallway the number on the door was 1200. "Let's go!" Alcena said, she took Abderus hand and pulled him out of the room. The doors then closed.

"Oh fine, now tell me, what kind of a mess have you gotten us into this time!" he said indignantly.

They walked slowly down the corridor and finally arrived at a door with the number 1212 on it the name under the number said 'The Antiquarian Brotherhood'. Alcena, in a bold move, opened the door, and walked through, dragging Abderus behind her. They were in a bright room with paintings on the wall and a comfortable looking place where cushions were encased in a structure of some kind. They walked over and sat down on the cushions. Alcena motioned to Abderus to be quiet. No one else was in the room. They looked around and saw paintings on the wall, but they weren't Hieroglyphics, they were drawings of men, and women in frames-they all looked very austere, and none of them were smiling.

"Why don't we just leave, there's nobody here, let's go out into the hallway to that cubicle room, and press the 'one' button, and ride it down!" Abderus said.

"No," said Alcena, "we must see this through to its conclusion." Suddenly a woman walked through a door to the right, holding a sheaf of papers, with glasses perched on the edge of her nose. She was dressed in black-she walked over to a desk piled with papers, added the papers that she had to the papers on the desk, and then looked up at the couch, and saw the children.

"What...children! What are you doing here?" She eyed them suspiciously, noting their clothing. "Do you have an appointment?"

"No," Alcena said, not knowing what an 'appointment' was, "we don't have an 'appointment'. We're here to see the boss!"

"The boss, you say," she smiled, "well the boss is in an important meeting, and he can't be disturbed."

"Just tell him that Alcena and Abderus are here, and they're very angry!"

Her smile disappeared. She stared at them, shook her head, and said, "Wait here, I'll be right back, they're all in a meeting now, and this is highly irregular." She went back to the door, opened it and left them alone.

"Well, now you've gone and done it, Miss Detective-what now?"

"You heard Anka, this must be played out!"

A few more minutes went by, and then the door opened and the woman walked out.

"They will see you now, but this is unexpected and highly irregular!" She kept the door open, and they both got up from the cushion contraption. Abderus sighed, and followed Alcena. She smiled at the woman, said "thank you," and they both proceeded through the door.

Chapter Twenty-Three... The Antiquarian Brotherhood

The children walked into what could be described as a typical Board Room, except that about eighteen men were seated on what appeared to be throne-like chairs, and the chairs were arranged in a triangle. Each chair seemed to have a pedestal with a screen attached to it- numbers and letters seemed to float beneath the screen. There was one other person in the room-he sat on a throne in the center of the triangle- He also had a screen with floating numbers and letters. His back was toward Alcena and Abderus. He turned his head around and appraised them, then he stood up and faced them.

"Gentlemen, may I introduce you to Alcena and Abderus, the daughter and son of Theoclea, the Delphic

Oracle, and the great Pythagoras." He smiled at them and shook his head in wonder. There were whispers, and loud talk that came from all parts of the triangle of men. 'The Boss' held up his hands to quiet them all.

"Quiet, everyone please!" he said.

"I know that this has been a busy day for all of us!"

"Young man and young woman, I am amazed at your ingenuity in finding us!"

"It wasn't that hard, Alcena said, you see, I'm a detective...and well, he protects me!"

Abderus shook his head in agreement, but did not say a word.

"Gentlemen, let me tell you about these children, Alcena is a singer-she writes her own songs, and they are quite good. Abderus is a writer, he writes poetry and verse that is way beyond his years, I've seen it. They are both about 13 to 15 years old, am I right?"

"Right,' they both said at the same time.

"How do you know so much about us?" Alcena said.

"Well, we already knew about you, and a friend of yours visited us just before you came in, she's gone now, a woman in a wheelchair named Troyana. Your visit is the last piece of the puzzle. Children, may I ask why you are here?"

"Well, for one thing, we were in the desert, and fell into a trap made of three crystals..."Alcena proceeded to tell them the whole story, leaving nothing out. In the end she said, "and that's how we came here! You tried to kill us –you sent that Muhajihadeem to kill us."

There was silence in the room. The Boss had a very serious expression on his face. He looked around at the members. He said, "It's Morvan, he's out of control, I should have followed my instincts about having us deal with him-He's not the kind of a person that we usually deal with. We never sent a Muhjihadeem after you, they haven't existed for centuries. We don't work with assassins, we are a centuries-old institution, obeying all of the laws of twenty-third century Egypt. This is all Morvan's work! He sent the Muhajihadeem. We will cease all trading with him immediately!"

"Twenty-third century Egypt!" Abderus exclaimed!" He looked at Alcena, and smiled-"I'm beginning to like this mystery, now!"

"Children, we shall send you back to your time, moments before you fell into the Triangle Trap. Go back and be with your protectors. Come over to me." They approached him cautiously. Abderus looked all about the room. He saw that on a pedestal in front of one of the members there was a crystal in the shape of a Five-pointed Star, and on another pedestal, on the opposite side, in front of another member, there was another crystal of matching size and quality in the shape of an Egg. Behind 'The Boss' in front of another member was a pedestal with a crystal in the shape of a Sphere, also of matching size and quality. Abderus stopped, and pulled Alcena back.

Then, Abderus said, "You are standing in a Triangle of Protection, safety, even healing. Pythagoras has described this to me."

"Yes, children, Pythagoras was wise to tell you these things, Abderus, your father is a very wise man, well known to us in the twenty-third century."

"Alcena, not to be outdone by Abderus, said, "and my mother Theoclea, the Delphic Oracle, the Dragon Priestess of the Earth, is she known to you as well?" she said defiantly.

The Boss, and all of the members of the Brotherhood smiled.

"Yes, "Alcena, your mother, Theoclea, the Delphic Oracle, The Pythia, the Pythian Priestess is very well known to all of us, all over the Earth! I might add that both of you are known to us as well, but it would disturb the Acausal realm for me to say any more. Now quickly, children, others are looking for you, join me in the triangle."

They joined him in the triangle, and he was in tears. "It has been my honor, and an honor for all of us to meet you. I only wish that the conditions had been less disruptive to you." He hugged both of them and stepped outside of the triangle. Instantly, the children were back at the edge of the fertile savannah. As they both walked back to their tent. Alcena said,

"Did you hear that! In the future we will both be well known, probably because of our skills as detectives in solving mysteries!"

"Don't get a big head about this, Alcena," Abderus replied, "he probably said that just to make us feel good."

They heard Morain and Panelle calling for them, they were standing in front of the tent. Morain and Panelle saw them, and they all hugged each other.

Alcena said, "Trust me, you wouldn't believe where we've been!"

"Yes, said Abderus proudly, "we've been in a Mystery that you would hardly believe!"

Chapter Twenty-Four... The trip to Luxor

The children were back at their tent, being tended to by Morain and Panelle. They told Morain and Panelle everything. The look on Theoclea's face when they next saw her showed that she knew very well what was going on. She sighed and said, "This all must play itself out"- then she told them of her plans to visit Luxor. Morain and Panelle were skeptical about Theoclea's trip, but Pythagoras assured them that when it came to protecting himself and Theoclea in Egypt, he was well suited to the task. He also asked Vorios to stay with the children, too. He wanted them to be well protected. Pythagoras and Theoclea left for Luxor, but Pythagoras suddenly had an uneasy feeling about the trip, a foreboding perhaps.

Eimon and Miriam had invited them, and met them at the Temple. They all explored Luxor, and then entered the Central Chamber of the Temple. Pythagoras, Theoclea, Eimon, and Miriam looked all about, while Eimon told them the stories behind some of the hieroglyphics. Pythagoras was looking for something else. He noted that there was a serpent on one of the walls-a scorpion on another- a black scarab, as well as other animals.

He was vaguely aware of Eimon's explanations. Pythagoras kept looking, something was wrong. He had his wand and staff with him, and also had three crystals in his pocket, a five–pointed star, a sphere, and an egg. All of these crystals were proportionately correct and even their translucent qualities matched.

Then he saw it, lying in front of the middle of one of the walls of the room, the wall to his right, a pentagon-shaped crystal on the ground. He looked at the opposite wall and saw that there was a crystal in the shape of a tetrahedron lying against the wall and it was proportionate in size and quality to the first! He knew what he would see lying in the middle of the floor of the wall opposite them. He took out his wand and walked over. Yes an obelisk-shaped crystal was placed toward the wall in the center. Pythagoras walked backwards toward the women, who were still discussing the hieroglyphics. He knew that the three crystals belonged to Morvan. Slowly, he walked over to the pentagon. He took out his five pointed star-shaped crystal and held it high as if absorbing its' energy, then placed it down about three feet in front of the pentagon. He whispered some words, one of which was 'past'.

The women stopped and noticed that he was doing something. Pythagoras walked over to the opposite wall and seemed to be drawing energy from the five-pointed star. He took out a spherical-shaped crystal, and placed it three feet from the tetrahedron. He seemed to be drawing energy from the star to the sphere. He whispered some words, one of which was 'present'.

Pythagoras looked back at the women, and said firmly-"Stand still, don't move!" He then walked back to the wall behind the women, and placed his egg-shaped crystal against the wall, directly opposite the obelisk- shaped crystal, whispering some words, one of which was 'future'. Once more, he returned to the five pointed star-shaped crystal and bowed to it. He stood in front of the women, his wand and staff were ready. They all were astounded when light beams shot from the pentagon, to the tetrahedron to the obelisk, and back to the pentagon. A triangle of light was formed. Pythagoras pointed his wand at the five–pointed star that had been placed against the wall, and a light beam shot out of it, hit the sphere, and then sought the egg, only to return to the five-pointed star.

They were encased in a triangle made of light beams-he was ready. Miriam, Eimon, and Theoclea stood together to his right. Suddenly, Morvan appeared in the other triangle, and Priori stood next to him with a worried look on her face. She was shocked and confused. She said,

"Morvan, why...?"

He said, "Shut up and stay out of this!" His attention went back to Pythagoras.

"Pythagoras, I see that you've put up the 'Triangle of Protection', a wise move, you old rascal. We have no need for these triangles-this is between us! I tried to scare those children so that you all would leave, but obviously it didn't work. Now I wish that they had died." Priori was in shock. She just stood there trying to process what was happening. Theoclea looked at her.

Pythagoras knew that Morvan was talking, trying to tap his emotions, that was his pattern. Pythagoras pointed to a picture of a scorpion on one of the hieroglyphics and fired at it with his wand, and suddenly, there was a huge scorpion in front of Morvan, making menacing moves toward him. Morvan stopped talking, looked at the hieroglyphics, found a scorpion on the opposite wall, and with his wand scratched out the scorpion's image in the hieroglyphic. The scorpion in front of him disappeared.

"Ah, Pythagoras, I see that you have not forgotten your tricks, but I fear that you've been hanging out with that Witch- Theoclea for too long." As he said that, Morvan was glancing around the room. 'More talk-trying to confuse me' thought Pythagoras. Morvan found it- a large black scarab, and pointed his wand at it. The scarab appeared in front of Pythagoras-it was hideous and menacing. Pythagoras looked about, found a black scarab on a wall, pointed his wand at it, and it disappeared.

"Pythagoras, I'm impressed, you remember all of your old tricks. I would have thought that hanging around all of those low-life Greeks would have weakened your wits."

Pythagoras knew what Morvan was going to do next. Morvan had his staff in his hand. Pythagoras quickly picked up his staff, ignored Morvan's chatter, and at the same time, both of them threw their staffs on the ground. The staffs immediately became two large pythons ready

211

to fight to the death. They hissed, spat and glared at each other, then attacked each other mercilessly. They twisted around each other, each trying to squeeze the life out of the other. After a few minutes of this, Morvan raised his wand and the pythons dropped and became staffs again. Both men retrieved their staffs.

"Obviously a stalemate so far," Morvan said, as he backed up and pulled a shocked Priori close to him. "But there's more, Pythagoras. Here's something that you were not taught in our classes." Pythagoras once again ignored his chatter. He motioned toward the women to stand back a few paces, and he did the same. Then, the 'Triangle of Destruction' that Morvan had made started to move forward toward the 'Triangle of Protection' that Pythagoras had created. Pythagoras said something to his staff, and his triangle advanced. When they touched each other, they continued to advance until a six-pointed star had been created, and then, the star obliterated itself. Nothing was left of the triangles.

"Another stalemate," Morvan said, "I congratulate you." Priori was wide eyed, and stared at Theoclea.

"I didn't want to do this, but I will have to," Morvan said. Priori shouted, "No, what are you doing?" He took out the 1849 Colt revolver pulled back the metal piece, and fired a ball point blank at Theoclea!

Chapter
Twenty-Five...Miriam

Suddenly, the scene froze, as if...and Theoclea could see the ball, aimed at her, frozen in the frame of black and white. Sonja appeared, drew her crystal weapon, and fired it, but the shot was blocked by some sort of a magic shield in front of Morvan. "Aura", a voice called-"The Fear, the Confusion"-Aura appeared and sent out fear and confusion to Morvan, but it was also blocked by a shield that he had put up. Axcelotl suddenly appeared, stepped in front of Theoclea, and made the 'sign of Eleusis' to stop the ball. Then, instantly the light and color came back to the scene, and Morvan pulled back the metal part, turned and fired the weapon point blank at Eimon, but at the first sign of trouble, Miriam had quickly moved in front of Eimon –Miriam was hit.

Theoclea saw the ball that was fired at her lying on the floor, and ran over to Miriam to see what she could do. Morvan grabbed Priori and shoved her in front of him as Pythagoras raised his Wand.

"I warn you, Pythagoras-I have shields up, your magic is useless. I can kill everyone in this room with this gun."

He pulled back the metal piece once more.

Priori and Theoclea exchanged quick glances. Priori twisted herself around to face him.

"You won't be killing anyone else with that thing." He pointed the gun at her and pulled the trigger. She laughed. "You've shot four of the balls at a target, and fired twice more today. There are no more balls in that thing! I never thought that you use it on people. You'll never use it again." She had palmed a knife in her hand, and stabbed him with it, not just once, but several times. He pulled the metal piece once more, and tried to pull the trigger-but blood was staining his robe-and his eyes rolled back. He slumped to his knees and said "You..." and then fell to the floor. He was dead.

Theoclea rushed over to Miriam-she was doing all that she could to help Miriam, but it was too late, the wound was a death wound. Miriam motioned to the pouch, and said to Theoclea-"The Medallion". Theoclea then reached into the pouch and took out the Medallion of Axcelotl, with Axcelotl's face and the crown of three crystals.

"I will return it," Miriam said, and her eyes rolled back.

Quickly, Axcelotl, Sonja, and Aura appeared in white ghostly forms. Miriam's Auric body left her dead body, and Axcelotl took her hand.

"You must go with us now, child." Theoclea rose, and gave Axcelotl the medallion. It shone with a radiant white light. Miriam was reassured by Aura's empathy, and Sonja's quiet singing. Axcelotl looked at the Medallion, and said, "Miriam, you have in an unfortunate way, fulfilled your mission, my child, you have returned the medallion to its' rightful owner." With that the three 'Spirits of Vigilance', and Miriam slowly became amorphous lights that drifted through the walls, on their way to the Sphere of the Moon.

Theoclea continued to listen to the singing and their whispers. She comforted Eimon who was shocked and in tears. "Listen Eimon," she whispered. "Miriam has to go with them." Eimon too, heard the whispers and the singing. She comforted Priori as well, who was confused and shocked.

"He never told me what was going to happen, I just thought that we were going to Luxor. I always keep the knife with me." With that, she collapsed into Theoclea's arms, sobbing. *You did what I told you to do, Priori, in the end, you did not follow him.*

215

Chapter Twenty-Six... The Eulogy to a Great Woman

Miriam, in a document that Eimon had been given, stipulated that she wanted a plain Jewish funeral, and that she preferred not to be embalmed, but to be buried, or placed in a tomb in a plain casket. It was to be done in a short time after her death. Her wishes were being respected. She would be placed in a special tomb reserved for heroes of Egypt. There were many people who knew that she had taken the shot meant to kill Eimon. There were many people who came to pay their last respects for she was well loved by the Egyptian people. Her casket was surrounded by a bed of roses. Theoclea's entire entourage was there, including the children. All of the proprieties of the funeral had been observed.

All that was left was the eulogy. It was among the last things to be done that night. Eimon walked gently up the steps to the casket and bed of Roses, and walked over to a lectern. She faced the Priests and Priestesses, Theoclea's entourage, the honored citizens of Egypt and all of the other guests from the many lands that traded with Egypt. Many of them had come for Theoclea's speech and had stayed in Egypt. She then invited Theoclea to come up the steps and stand beside her. Tears welled up in her eyes, but she fought them back, looked down, and composed herself.

"May my sister's name 'Miriam', be forever engraved in our hearts, and the hearts of all men and women who have been touched by her steadfastness and loyalty." Eimon was in tears, and Theoclea reached out and gave her a cloth to wipe them away. She gratefully accepted it.

She used the cloth, and then continued.

"It is rare for someone of her talents to pass our way. We have all been enriched by the beauty of her soul, the compassion of her heart. Blessed be to my sister, Miriam. We have all been blessed as we have met her, on our paths. Blessed Be to Miriam! She helped so many, and her compensation often was just a few kind words. She expected little, and gave so much. She saved my life..."-she burst into tears, but then composed herself-she knew that she had to continue."

"May her life be an example to all of us. She forgave, she understood. Blessed Be to Miriam!"

"Miriam was my Protector. She assumed that role of her own accord, of her own free will. I will not go into the details of this, but in the end I learned that she guarded a great treasure as well, something that was given to her by her father. In the end, Miriam, at the moment of her death delivered the treasure to its' rightful owner, the spirit that guided her through the transition to death."

"Miriam requested that should anything happen to her, she preferred to have a funeral arranged quickly, according to the laws of Judaism, and that she be buried without the usual Egyptian proprieties, and we are honoring her wishes today." Eimon then turned to Theoclea, and said,

"Miriam told me that in the short time that she knew you, she felt like a sister to you. She told me that she was very inspired by your speech. She told me that she had read your book, and that it had been a pivotal moment in her life. I wrote the words down that she wanted to say to you, Theoclea, not knowing that it would be part of her Eulogy.

She used the cloth once more to wipe away her tears. "This is what she said to me, Theoclea."

"Theoclea gave us glimpses into the future and the past. Her magic will not be forgotten. To all of those in the future who learn about her, or hear her voice in their minds, or read about who she was and what she did, we say, you too are blessed. For a 'Dear One' came our way, and she will surely touch you as well. Her speech will live on in our memories, and our hearts. So gifted, so joyful in the face of adversity, always ready to give encouragement, and to share her visions and prophecies. She is not just the eyes and ears of Greece, she is the eyes and ears of our world, of the past, present, and future. She spoke not just to us, but to those in the future as well."

Theoclea reached out to Eimon and embraced her. She then stood beside her as Eimon continued.

"Blessed Be to our Dear One, Miriam! She passed our way, and now has left us. Her memory will caress us and stay with us until our dying days. We have all been blessed by knowing her. We would all be less had we not known her. We say goodbye to our dear one. Perhaps, in another life, or another place, or time we may meet her again. Hopes of that kind persist in our minds, and console us. Goodbye Miriam, my sister. We laughed, we cried, we talked of many things, we argued as sisters do, and we parted, only to talk again. We all shared a piece of Miriam's life, it seems like such a brief time. I can honestly say in the end, that for all of it, after the laughter and the tears, we are better for having known you, Miriam, my sister. We are all better for having your spirit touch us. Blessed Be, Miriam, Blessed Be." She broke down, sobbing. Theoclea held her in her arms, crying as well. Morain gave them both handkerchiefs, and sent them waves of empathy. Panelle guarded the casket-she wanted no more trouble on this trip. She glanced over at Priori, who fainted at the sight of all of this.

"...man feels directly and indirectly on all the Kingdoms, and thus enters into constant exchange with their particular natures, and finally, by way of their mineral origin (bones), with the cosmic energy from which everything arises."...R.A. Schwaller de Lubicz

'Every cell pulsates, absorbs, reflects and interacts with the acoustic oscillations of the medium."... Guiliana Conforto

"Across planes of consciousness, we have to live with the paradox that opposite things can simultaneously be true"...Ram Das

"The golden light of a candle flame sits upon the throne of its dark light that clings to the wick"...I bring you words from the Zohar.

Chapter Twenty-Seven...Theoclea and The Book

... While on the floats,
there were statues
of the
great beasts from the East
with their trunks held high
squirting water at the sky,
In a fine display of water play
that will not be equaled until the day
When the pond and the tree
have had their final say...

She sat on the edge of her bed, dressed in a white robe-she had told Pythagoras that on that night she wanted to be alone, and he respected that. Theoclea stared at the book, lying on a table.

She knew what she had to do. She walked over to the book, placed her hands on it, paused a moment and sighed. Then, she picked it up and walked out of the tent into the night.

She knew where she had to go-to the pond and the bench. It was a clear night, and a full moon lit the way. She walked, holding the book close to her. Finally, she arrived at the bench, sat down, and placed the book beside her.

Theoclea picked up two stones and threw them into the pond. Moments later, moonlit reflections appeared on the branches of the tree, moving from the ends of the smallest branches on the right inward toward the trunk, and then outward toward the smallest ends of the branches on the left. This time, though, there were little circles, like stars moving against a fixed starry moonlit background. Her attention was abruptly drawn to her right and she saw the solemn procession of Priests and Priestesses-each one holding a candle. One of them was playing a heartbeat on a drum. She heard their chanting and smelled their incense.

All of a sudden, one of the Priestesses turned and looked at her. She was not smiling. It was Hatshepsut, only this time, she left the procession, and walked toward Theoclea. The drumming stopped, and all of the

Priestesses and Priests turned and looked at Theoclea. When Hatshepsut arrived at the bench, she saw the book, and said, "You know what you must do!"

Slowly, Hatshepsup's visage and clothing blurred, and to Theoclea's astonishment, she saw Aura standing in Hatshepsut's place. Aura executed a quick dance move, spun around, put her hands together and made the "Gate of Eleusis" gesture, a horrified look on her face. She pointed her hands at the book. Theoclea closed her eyes and saw the mental images that Aura wanted her to see. There were scenes of unimaginable horror and destruction, and the implication was that the reason for the painful scenes that she saw was in the book. She opened her eyes with the realization that the ideas and formulas in the book would be used for destructive purposes-a living nightmare. She looked at the spot where Aura had been, but she had disappeared.

Theoclea turned to the book on her left, and without delay, she picked it up. She knew what she had to do. She stood up and went over to the stone stairway that led down to the pond, and made her way down. When she arrived at the bottom of the stairway she walked over and sat on the rock. She heard singing and looked up at the bench. Sonja was standing there on the edge of the cliff face singing, and Aura was next to her dancing slowly. At that point, she saw all of the members of the solemn procession-the Priests and Priestesses lined up on the edge of the cliff, each one holding a candle.

They were all chanting, and the drummer was playing the heartbeat. The singing, chanting and drumming continued. Theoclea looked at the pond, saw the sparkling lights silhouetted in the moonbeams, and observed the green lights approaching her under the water, but never reaching her. She took the book and placed it on another rock. The singing and the chanting continued. Gusts of wind entered-they blew the book open and the pages flipped back and forth as the wind circled and picked up speed. She looked up at the tree, and saw that it seemed to be lit up as if thousands of fireflies had settled on its' branches. The pages of the book flipped back and forth. The chanting, drumming, singing and dancing continued.

Theoclea heard thunder, looked up at the sky, and all of a sudden, a lightning bolt appeared from the South and struck the book. Almost immediately, another bolt came from the opposite direction and struck the book a second time. Smoke from the burning book rose quickly into the sky forming a cloud. Then, two lightning bolts came from the East and the West, and crossed under the cloud-It was her sign, the sign of the Delphic Oracle.

Even though the book had been struck twice, some of it still remained. The cloud glowed as if it had absorbed the energy of the lightning. The chanting, drumming, the dancing of Aura, and the singing of Sonja continued. Then, Theoclea noticed that the green lights under the water in the pond were slowly approaching her as before. As they approached, they rose to the surface. When they reached the surface, each one shot a stream of water from the pond about six feet into the air. They were first a reddish color, and soon after, they changed to orange-the music of Pythagoras' poem was heard-it was very loud.

A dub-dub step-step
crunching all around
In a myriad of beats,
A cacophony of sound-
The music encircled her
Going round and round

Theoclea glanced at the top of the cliff face-the chanting, drumming, dancing of Aura, and singing of Sonja continued.

The effect on the pond was like a fountain. There must have been over a hundred green lights that now became part of a huge fountain. The water had gone from red to orange to yellow as some of the water jets became lower, and some went higher. Patterns were made that seemed to echo the dub-dub, step-step music. The jets of water rose higher, some turning pink, and others turning green.

There was a whirling of pink and green water blown around by the gusts of air, that swiftly changed to blue. On the cliff, Sonja was singing higher and higher notes. The blue changed to violet as the water jets in the center rose higher and higher with Sonja's notes. All at once, Sonja sang a high note of exquisite clarity and tone-the highest note that she was capable of. One jet in the center rose all of the way up, and hit the cloud that had been caused by the lightning and burning of the book.

It started to rain, first a circle of rain lit by a white light-and before long, the circle widened. Torrents of rain came down, lit by an ever widening circle of white light. The torrential downpour lasted for some time. What remained of the book was drenched, and Theoclea's white robe was drenched as well. Slowly, the rain and the dub-dub, step-step music receded somewhat, and things got quieter. The rain quieted down to a drizzle.

Theoclea stood up, the rain mingling with her tears. Before long, the rain slowly stopped, but the singing, chanting drumming and dancing continued. Theoclea saw that all of the small and medium sized stones all around her started to rise. There were hundreds of them, perhaps thousands of them, and they rose slowly while the chanting and drumming continued. She looked up at the cliff and saw that Sonja and Aura had stopped, and were watching the stones with concerned looks on their faces.

Without warning, the chanting and drumming stopped, and the stones started to hurl themselves at the book. Many of the stones hit Theoclea, for in its' acts of destruction the Earth is indiscriminate. Theoclea was in pain, and bleeding all over. The rain of stones continued, she was struck again and again by more stones. One of them struck her in the head, knocking her unconscious as more and more stones continued to hit her and the book. The book was reduced to tiny pieces that were being washed into the pond by the rainwater. The stones continued to hit Theoclea. This went on for an indeterminate length of time. Finally, Theoclea breathed her last breath, the fire of life went out inside of her, her heart stopped, and her blood stopped circulating. She lay silently on the rock. She was dead.

Chapter Twenty-Eight...Death and The Gate

She was dead. Her body was soaked in water and blood. She lay there in the rainwater, her blood mixing with the water-and then, suddenly the scene was frozen as if...and Axcelotl appeared wearing a golden crown of three crystals. She saw what had happened to Theoclea. She saw the stones frozen in the air. Dark figures were appearing. She made the sign of the Gate of Eleusis.

"No, not my daughter-NO NOT HER!" she shouted!

She knelt down, tears in her eyes. She took off the golden crown, and gently placed it on Theoclea's head. Then, she closed her eyes and started to chant in a language that had not been spoken for thousands of years. The tears continued to pour from her eyes as she touched Theoclea's blood- soaked body. The golden crown was becoming soaked in blood from the head wounds. Slowly, ever so slowly, the blood and wounds around the crown of three crystals started to slowly disappear. Axcelotl touched all of the chakras of Theoclea's body. Theoclea's pulse and heartbeat slowly experienced 'renewal', but could barely be felt. Axcelotl kept chanting, as she gently removed the Crown, washed it in the pond, and placed it back on Theoclea's head. Theoclea had still not risen to consciousness.

The head wound was serious. The book was shattered to pieces, beyond recognition. Axcelotl placed her hands together and made the sign of The Gate of Eleusis once again. Then all was blackness, as if they were somewhere out in the cosmos. There was a small pinpoint of light that shone on Theoclea's unconscious blood stained body, as if one star was shining in a coal black sky. Slowly the pinpoint widened, and color was coming back to the scene. One by one the stars started to shine again, and one by one the wounds on Theoclea's body slowly healed. She still wore the golden crown, and lay unconscious on the rock.

When the stars had all come back, Theoclea's mind slowly rose to consciousness. Once again, an indeterminate length of time had gone by. An unexpected 'resurrection' had occurred, perhaps only foreseen by the Goddess Ma'at, for Ma'at is the unseen ground of our existence on this plane. Ma'at is the appearance of the unexpected synchronicity. Theoclea felt her head, and carefully removed the golden crown, the pain and the head wounds were gone. She stared at the crown and then placed it back on her head. She felt her body-there was no pain, and all of the wounds were almost healed. She looked up at the cliff face and saw that Sonja and Aura were gone. The solemn procession of the Priests and Priestesses was gone as well. Her clothes were soaked in blood and water. She looked over and the book was gone.

Looking toward her right, at the edge of the pond, she saw The gate of Eleusis, its' shining crystal lanterns trailing down from it. The Guardian was standing next to the gate, dressed in a striped robe of ochre, russet, olive, and black. His arms were folded and he was holding something-a violet robe. He looked over and smiled at Theoclea, then walked about twenty feet away, and stood there, staring at the stars. Theoclea staggered to a standing position, slowly walked over to the gate pole, and leaned her head and shoulder against it. The familiar feeling that she had had twice before-at Eleusis-and on Atlantis- came rushing through her. It was a torrent of joy and strength. She allowed this to surge through her for an unmeasured length of time, savoring the feeling. Finally she stood straight, moved back from the gate pole and smiled at the guardian. She saw that he was holding a violet robe. He walked toward her and said,

"Theoclea, you have reached the third and final Gate. You have faced your own death, and you have fulfilled your mission. Here is a gift for you-the violet robe." He handed the robe to her, she looked at it and thanked him. He smiled a benign smile, turned around and said, "Take off the blood-stained white robe, and put on the violet robe." She did what he asked her to do, and stood there, with the blood-stained white robe on the ground. After a minute, he turned around and picked up the blood-stained robe. He admired the golden crown of three crystals that she wore. "Axcelotl has several crystal crowns, but rarely wears the golden one, and she has given it to you-the highest honor," he said.

"Theoclea, you have left your fingerprint on the final Gate. It is time to go through-this is the last Gate, and there are wonders to be seen. She felt a hint of fear, but he reassured her. He held her hand, and led her through the last gate…She saw many wondrous things…She saw The Light of Truth. She saw the Source of all things, the essence that unifies everything that seems separate and unconnected. She saw the Gods and Goddesses as...simply one. She saw the creation of the Pentacle and the Rose, the creation of the KeyRose box, the creation of the gold, black, and red keys, and in the end experienced a revelation concerning a great wheel of the cosmos-a final understanding-it all made sense...and much more...then...slowly a strange sleep came upon her.

The Light

I gazed into the Light
Of Truth itself
What I saw in that light is
beyond the ability of words to describe
In its' depths I saw all of the elements of the Universe
That seem separate and scattered
united into one place,
bound together and connected by Love
Substance; accidents; synchronicities; events; emotions
everything intertwined.
I saw the universal form that fuses all things
Anyone who sees the light is transformed
I saw the Gods and Goddesses eternal and unchanged
simply one.
Then I saw three circles all the same size,
but of different colors,
each reflecting the other
like a rainbow within a rainbow
They coalesced and I saw the image of the sun with

a mortal inside of it.

The sun changed into a gold-colored basket.

The mortal changed into a dark five-pointed star...

A Pentacle was formed.

Slowly, one by one four roses appeared between the points

with one space vacant

Then I saw two keys in the vacant space.

A gold key and a black key

The gold key and black key dissolved, and I saw

A box with a red key on top.

The box opened to reveal a black cloth, and there were pieces in the box.

The box then disappeared and I was left with

The gold-colored basket, the dark metal star and the roses

The Pentacle and the Rose

and then...

Suddenly it came to me

in a flash of light,

and I understood completely

A perfectly balanced wheel had been set in motion,

driven by the love that moves

The Sun, Moon, and Stars

Panorpheus, with thanks to Dante Alighieri...2007

Chapter Twenty-Nine...Theoclea Awakens

Theoclea woke up in bed, still in Egypt. She looked around. The book was gone, and her wet blood-soaked white robe was draped over a chair. On the seat of the chair was the golden crown of three crystals. It all came back to her. She was wearing the violet robe. She took it off and looked all over herself for any wounds. All of the wounds had healed. She then noticed that there was a symbol on the back of the robe-it was the Pentacle and the Rose symbol, in gold, black, and red. She smiled and put the robe on again. Morain knocked on the door.

"Theoclea, are you awake? We're leaving today." Theoclea looked in a mirror...there were no wounds on her face...she started to cry.

"Morain," she said, "please come in."

Morain entered, and quickly surveyed the scene. The blood-stained robe,-Theoclea in tears-the new violet robe that she was wearing- The crown of three crystals, and then she saw that The Book was gone. She walked over and embraced Theoclea, then looked at her hands. She held Theoclea's hands, and they both closed their eyes, their minds melded, their eyes were closed. Morain saw it all-Theoclea sitting on the bench with the book, Aura showing her the vision- The chanting and drumming of the Priests and Priestesses in the solemn procession, their candles flickering in the breeze. She heard the singing of Sonja, and saw the dancing of Aura. She saw the tree, the pond, the stars-she saw it all. She saw the stones wounding Theoclea-she saw Theoclea lying dead on the rock. Then she saw Axcelotl appear and stop it all. Theoclea's wounds that healed; The Gate; The Guardian in the multi-colored robe; the gift, and Theoclea being led through the gate. She saw it all. Then they both opened their eyes.

Theoclea turned around to show the back of the robe. Morain stared at the symbol on the robe that the Guardian had given Theoclea. She sensed that Theoclea's tears were tears of joy, mixed with hope.

"The 'renewal', Morain, it cannot be stopped now. I must rest. I want to tell the others. Please ask Vorios, and Pythagoras, Panelle and The Scribe to come here at once." Morain walked out and quickly gathered the others. As they all walked back to Theoclea's bedchamber, she related the events that Theoclea had shared with her, omitting nothing.

When they arrived at Theoclea's bedroom, they quietly walked in. She was asleep. They all looked at the blood-stained white robe and noticed the new violet robe that she wore. They saw the crown of three crystals lying on the chair. There was silence, and then The Scribe spoke:

"Through Aura's vision, Theoclea saw the horrors that would occur if the book fell into the wrong hands-and most assuredly, it would have. She made a brave decision. She walked into the storm rather than avoid it."

"She received the wounds. Already my sight is starting to fail again. She gave me the gift of seeing and remembering." He looked at Vorios, and the others, and said,

"She received the wounds, she braved the stigmata and faced her own death. Her blood-stained white robe is proof of this. Then the gate appeared once more-she met the final Guardian, and touched the final Gate. He then led her through the Gate. Who knows what wondrous things that she saw! We have witnessed a great achievement here-for there are few who walk through. Very few have accomplished this."

"Through Theoclea's words-we have seen her growth-from a child who had her first vision-saw the Gate of Eleusis and the Guardian-to the woman who shared her wisdom at Eleusis, where she touched the gate the first time. I met her, as The Grandfather on Atlantis. She met the Lady in White, and was given the gift of being a healer. She touched the gate a second time, and saved the Guardian's life."

"She saw the destruction of Atlantis, and now, in Egypt, she has touched a huge number of people with her words and thoughts. She has touched the final Gate, and can proudly wear the violet robe. The Pentacle and the Rose was one of the first gifts that was given to her by Pythagoras, shortly after she became The Oracle."

"She has now fulfilled the task given to her at least 700 years ago by Orpheus. We have come full circle, she has seen the promise of her destiny, she has met the final Guardian, in the multi-colored robe, and has given us the gift- "The Triumph of the Rose.""

No one said a word, waiting to hear if he had more to say. He thought privately to himself-'*I remember now-It was only my copy of the book, I'm glad that she knew to give it back to the Elements, for the book posed a great danger. I know where the original book is, but the secret will die with me, perhaps to be revealed by me in another incarnation, thousands and thousands of years from now, when the time is right, and the book will...*' He then forgot the rest of what he was thinking, for the blindness was quickly coming back. Suddenly he had a last revelation, and said,

"I remember-I remember!

I was Orpheus!

I gave Theoclea the task, and my dream and vision of

the unity

Of the Dark and the Light,

Dionysus, and Apollo

in the one temple!

I was Orpheus!

I stopped the blood sacrifice in the Temples

I wrote the invocations that were used at

The Mysteries of Eleusis

I put the treasure box together

I gave her the Rose Medallion

Of the Goddess, Inanna

To balance the two Gods!

243

I gave her the Keys, and the KeyRose box
I gave her the parchment that
described 'The Pentacle and the Rose'
I was Orpheus!
He looked at her one last time, and there were tears in
his eyes
I was Orpheus!
She has fulfilled her vow to me!
I was Orpheus!

With that, his sight and memory failed. Vorios, Panelle, and Morain helped him as he sank to his knees.

Pythagoras quietly went up to Theoclea, still asleep in her bed, he looked at the blood stained robe, and kneeled down by the side of the bed. He lightly touched her face, and she woke up. "Pythagoras, I've been asleep-she looked around the room, and saw the blood-stained white robe, Vorios, Morain, Panelle and The Scribe.

She looked at The Scribe and sadly noted that his blindness had returned, and his memory had receded. She had known all along that this would eventually happen, but she was not prepared for the sadness that briefly entered her heart.

"What has been happening?" she said.

244

"Theoclea, much has happened in this room-there were revelations…you're tired, you must rest. We will all tell you what has happened, but you must rest now-he looked over at the blood-stained robe and the golden crown.

She turned around and showed everyone the symbol on the back of the violet robe, 'The Pentacle and the Rose'. She saw the crown of three crystals on the chair, then turned around to face them and said, "He gave the violet robe to me after I touched the gate! He was dressed in a multicolored robe of ochre, russet, olive and black." There were tears in her eyes, and Morain walked over and gave her the handkerchief. She dried her eyes, looked at the handkerchief, and held it tightly.

Pythagoras said, "Axcelotl brought you back from death, and gave you the golden crown!"

"Yes," Theoclea said, as she held up her right hand that still held the handkerchief, and made a fist. "Then this is a moment for rejoicing-even celebration!"

Theoclea smiled at all of them, and said, "Why does everything that goes on with us, and the Temple of Delphi have to be so serious? We have the festival to prepare for! Please ask Anka, Troyana, and Bella to join us as soon as they can, at Delphi, and tell the Merchant to bring some special candles! The Scribe must join us this year as well. Eimon and Priori must meet Bella and her troupe!" The Scribe will be delighted by Demetrios' music, Reena's singing, the poetry and music of our children, and the singing of the orphan's choir, and he will be the guest of honor at the rituals and workshops." The Scribe smiled at this.

She laughed, and said, "This should be a moment of joy, I have fulfilled my vow to Orpheus!"

She laughed, and the others laughed with her. Morain walked over, and Theoclea handed her the handkerchief, saying "keep this for me, Morain." Morain nodded, she understood, and smiled.

'Well, what are we all waiting for? It's time to return to Delphi. The annual festival of the "Two Rituals of Balance" is only a couple of months away! The planning must start now, there is much to do!" Theoclea said.

Morain turned to Panelle, and both of them smiled proudly at each other, for it was their sacred responsibility to start the planning. Theoclea then motioned for Pythagoras to come closer to her. She whispered to him, so that the others would not hear her-

"Pythagoras, what would you think if I dyed my hair red, like Eimon's?"

Pythagoras smiled through his tears, then whispered back,

246

"Theoclea, I like your hair just the way it is."

He then kissed her passionately.

*So ends the story of Theoclea (The Delphic Oracle) and Pythagoras in Egypt. She was the Pythia; The Pythian Priestess; The Dragon Priestess of the Earth; The Delphic Oracle. She was a Priestess of Apollo and Dionysus, and unified the worship of both Gods in the Glorious Temple of Delphi. She also wore the Rose Medallion, the Token of Inanna. She was a follower of Inanna as well and felt that the Goddess was needed to provide balance with the Gods. Inanna's symbol was **The Rose**. Blessed Be, Theoclea*

PanOrpheus 2011

The Triumph of the Rose

I stared at the book
It was finished, I suppose,
But it needed something more
What was it...Who knows?
A fern in a moon-lit garden-
A silver-strewn strand with an
Opaline pearl?
A thought in the mind of a Spirit of old
More visions of the future from a
gifted young girl?
And then it came to me to me,
That in the mists that had risen
From the Tripod chair that Theoclea chose,
A flame had risen in me,
and guided my pen-

In such a Way
that the Path of my prose
was indeed-in the end-
The Triumph of The Rose.

A Poem by Abderus, the son of Theoclea (The Delphic
Oracle) and Pythagoras...age Twelve
From-
Theoclea (The Delphic Oracle)
Sees
Atlantis

The Dark Night of the Soul

I stood in a clearing
It was the midnight of my fortieth year
The forest was dark, and reflected the state that
my soul was in.
All my life I had followed a path,
The path of a man whose soul sought life's pleasures,
It was a path of solitude, for I had never married, never had
children, never had given myself to anyone in the way that
men pledge themselves to another.
I wandered about the clearing, as if in a dream, thinking of
all that had befallen me in the previous year.
The end of a love-
The loss of my dear Lady of Peace for whom I had almost
pledged myself-only to lose her to a prolonged illness.

250

My heart yearned for her, I felt incomplete, and my friend
and confidant was gone.

Music had always been an important element in my life.
I was a musician of great renown...once...and yet even
music did not move me as it once had.

My soul was out of balance-as if the Sacred Feminine and
the Sacred Masculine were ghosts, lost in a fog. The Gods
and the Goddesses had forsaken me and had allowed me to
stray from the path

A fleeting thought of ending it all passed through my mind,
when all of a sudden I saw an object on the path that was lit
by the full moon. Walking toward it, I saw that it was a rose
that had fallen from a nearby rose bush.

As I gazed at it in the moonlight, it seemed to speak to me- I
listened, and it said:

"Of all the paths that one must tread
(Before one departs for the land of the dead)
There is one on which you must pay the toll
And walk right through
The Dark Night of the soul.
And if by chance you might meet
someone
who gives you the rose when the night is done.
There is something here that you must say:
"With this rose in my heart I'll greet the new day"

251

I pondered these words, and then saw that another was

walking toward me.

Her soul was in darkness, but she could see

The hurt in my eyes,

The pain in my heart

The wound was still bleeding

I had taken life's dart

She picked up the rose and gave it to me,

saying

"I give you the rose to set your heart free."

And so my dear listener,

For that's who you are

I give you the rose

You have come from afar.

Your mind is troubled

Your heart is not free

The gift of this rose

I pass on to thee.

Lyrics of a song 'The Pentacle and the Rose'
By Alcena, the daughter of Theoclea (The Delphic oracle),
and Pythagoras...age Twelve
From-
Theoclea (The Delphic Oracle)
Sees
Atlantis

There's a Rose that grows in moonlight,
Its petals wait for dew.
On fern-braided trails,
In luminous veils
It's silver-sweet scent waits for you
It grows in lands of darkness below in wondrous gloom
On opaline threads in lush amber beds
It spreads its strange perfume.

Up above it blooms near night-shade, in diamond motes of
moon-beams
Where on the ground a Pentacle lies
Its' Poet-soul listens and dreams.

The Pentacle's a symbol
Of air, water, fire and earth
As everyone knows

It points to the Spirit
With the Rose
It shows its worth.

If you come upon the Roses,
And have the Pentacle too,
Watch out for the thorns
And join them together
The Pentacle and the Rose.

Addendum One
Theoclea in Eleusis

There is a 'prequel' to the book that you have just read. It's called "Theoclea (The Delphic Oracle) in Eleusis. All of the other characters, Pythagoras, Morain, Panelle, Vorios, Anka, Troyana, and others are introduced for the first time. Theoclea is to give a speech to the Pilgrims the night before 'The Mysteries' are going to start. She has waited a long time to give the speech. The suspense and the magic of a week in the 'tent city' all lead up to a speech that is tinged with the magic and the vision, the wisdom, and the unpredictable nature of Theoclea, our 'Delphic Oracle'.

I've included the First Chapter "Three Children."

"Midway in the journey
of this life,
I found myself
in a dark wood,
For I had lost
the Right Path"

Dante-the
Beginning of
"The Inferno"

1.

THREE CHILDREN

"Do you see that cloud in the sky?" Theoclea said, "It's pointing to the magic grove! There's the Pan statue, in the grass! Now I know that we're on the right path!"

Theoclea carefully led the way to a stand of trees, the others followed behind her. They were children, they were different, and they viewed the world with a heightened sense of wonder. They passed an empty donation urn, and peered into it. "I've been told to stay away from these urns, and never to touch one. They have spells on them!" Theoclea said.

It was a beautiful spring day and the ground was covered with moss-covered rocks. Theoclea picked up one of the rocks, put it in a fabric bag, and said "I have a new saying- if you pick up a rock, you must return and place three rocks on the same spot!"

" Theoclea- you're going to be a writer, the cards have told me that," said Troyana. Finally they entered a clearing ringed with pine trees. They approached the center, and Theoclea pointed ahead.

"Do you see that big standing stone? That's another marker-we're getting closer! There's the Treasure chest!" Theoclea said excitedly.

She pointed to an old chest that was in the middle of the grove. Hanging from the gold lock on the chest was a large red key. "That red key opens the chest," Theoclea said. "I opened it this morning and it was full of papers with pictures and symbols on them." Carefully, she took the red key, and inserted it into the lock. The lock opened and she lifted up the top of the chest. The two other girls looked on in wonder. "The papers are gone! It's full of clothing and other things. We can all dress up for the ritual!"

"Why do we have to dress up?" said Anka, "It's always hard to find the right things to wear when we do this."

"We have to dress up so that we can BE the Goddesses, you know that! Now today, Anka, you'll be Artemis! There's a bow and arrows in the trunk! Here's a white tunic that you can wear, too."

"Why can't I be Aphrodite, Theoclea, you always get the best part!"

"Alright, Anka, I know what you want, so let's let the stones decide!"

"Yes, the stones," Anka said, taking some stones of various colors out of her pocket. Bending down, the others joined her. She then rolled the stones on the ground, and shrieked with delight. "You see, the stones are saying that I shall be Aphrodite today, and you shall be Artemis!"

Troyana watched them, shaking her red hair.

"When will the two of you ever learn to stop fighting over these things, I have the best way." She took out some cards from her pocket with strange symbols that she had drawn on them. "You may think that I drew these yesterday, but you're wrong" she said in a low mysterious voice.

She motioned to Theoclea and Anka to be seated. They all sat down on the mossy-cool ground. Continuing in a low voice, Troyana said, "These are the cards of a Sybil, and only I know what they mean! The symbols come from Egypt, and they're very old!"

"Oh Troyana, we know that you drew these cards yourself," Anka said.

"Hush, little ones, these cards can read the past, present and future! I know this to be true!"

Theoclea thought for a moment. "Maybe we can use the cards in our ritual! Yes," Theoclea continued, "that's the spell we can work on, seeing into the future. Here's the chant, we have to practice it. Over and over we can say, 'It's starting, it's starting, it's starting'. We shall begin, of course with all of the proper things, just like they do at the Temple. The purification of the members, the dark invocations, the directions, and, well you know, all of that silly stuff! Then we'll dance and chant round and round, and *then* we'll look at the cards!"

"They don't do that at the Temple," said Troyana.

"How do *you* know?" said Theoclea. Do you see them in the clouds, like I do? Do you hear their whispers?"

"Here she goes", said Anka. "Calm down, Theoclea, it's only pretending."

"Pretending, you say, pretending, well how 'bout this, is this pretending?"

She stared at the stones on the ground intently, and nothing happened. Troyana looked doubtfully at Anka. Suddenly, Theoclea looked up and saw her friends as if they were frozen in time, as if a film projector had stopped, and only one frame of a black and white film could be seen.

She looked around and it seemed as if the daylight had disappeared, as if it were night. There was no breeze. She was sitting on the ground, with her friends, but they were frozen on the spot, looking at each other doubtfully. She looked around again, and knew that something was wrong. A sound broke the silence, a loud cracking sound, she faced the direction of the sound and saw a tree, and in an instant she *knew* that it was about to fall.

She looked at the others, frozen in the frame of black and white. She looked at the tree- it was frozen as well, but she had heard the sound and she *knew* that the tree would injure them. She *saw* the direction of its fall.

She looked up and there were vague crystal lights against a black sky. In an instant the light came back, and she grabbed both of her friends and screamed at them, pushing them away as hard as she could, and throwing all of her weight at them. The tree fell with a loud crack, and she blacked out. All was blackness, except for the amorphous light-shapes.

The room was cloudy. She was sitting on the chair, the one at the Temple, where the Oracle sat, she smelled the funny smell that came from the chamber. She wore the red key on a thong around her neck. She saw faces, she heard whispers. Then all was darkness. For a brief moment she saw a gate with white crystal lights flowing away from it. A man was standing near the gate. She touched the gate, then held her right arm out in a "come hither" gesture, her palm up.

She brought her left hand forward, and placed it directly over her right hand so that the thumb and all fingers touched. She folded over the middle fingers, so that only the thumbs, forefingers and little fingers were touching. Quickly, she brought both hands to an upright position, the hands still clasped, the fingers and the thumbs pointing upward. The sign looked like the gate. She then parted her hands, palms up, mimicking the flowing strands of white crystal light that flowed away from the gate. Then all was blackness.

Slowly a small circle of light appeared in the darkness. The light grew, until she heard familiar voices, and saw familiar faces. The light returned, and the clouds parted.

"Theoclea, are you all right?" Anka said.

"Theoclea, you saved us, then you fainted. What happened?" Troyana said. Tears appeared in Theoclea's eyes, and she started to cry, her eyes continuing to produce an outpouring of tears.

"Yes, Theoclea," Anka said, "what did you see? You saved us from the falling of the tree." She pointed at the tree that rested only a few feet away from them.

"What happened, Theoclea?" Troyana said once more.

Theoclea tried to hold back the tears, and when she finally calmed back down a bit, the crying stopped. She looked at both of her friends as if seeing them for the first time. Then she said,

"There was a tree, then, strange crystal lights in the sky. There was a room with the Oracle's chair in it. Then I saw…a gate with lights on it. A man was standing near the gate.

I touched the gate, and…I…did something with my hands…I think that I saw…the…the… *FUTURE!*"

Here are the first two chapters of the second Theoclea Book-Theoclea (The Delphic Oracle) sees Atlantis

1.

More Whispers

Theoclea looked out the window of her bedchamber. She saw a few birds, and they appeared to be flying across the moon, which was barely in the waxing crescent phase. She turned and sat down at her writing desk, and dipped her pen in the ink bottle. Her cat "Kitty" was nestled against her and sleeping.

"More Whispers" she wrote in big letters on the title page of a notebook. She looked satisfied with this, and then turned the page. She began writing again.

PROLOGUE

Many of you have read my first book, 'Whispers'. I am the Delphic Oracle, The Pythia, The Dragon Priestess of the Earth. My name is Theoclea. I live in the Temple of Delphi, and I am the first Oracle to have chosen to be both a Priestess of Apollo and Dionysus. I have the ability to see into the future as well as into the past. My powers have been growing, and each year I can see more. I had my first vision when I was a child, playing with friends. For two days a month, I sit on the Tripod Chair, in the subterranean chamber at the Temple of Delphi. The Dragon's breath comes up through cracks in the floor, I inhale the Dragon's Magic, and it helps me to go into a trance. I am asked questions, and the answers come to me through the God Apollo. Perhaps there are other Gods and Goddesses involved in the process as well.

I know that I am different. I have visions. The important thing here is that I consider *words* to be part of my Magical Gifts. I seem to know what to say, and do in many situations. I am grateful for the guidance and gifts that the Gods, the Goddesses and the Earth have given to me. I am grateful for my Protector, Panelle, and my

Counselor Morain. They help me when I faint or have other troubles. They're there for me.

There may be some of you who attended my speech to the Pilgrims the night before the Mysteries of Eleusis began a year ago. If you were there, you know that I quoted from my first book 'Whispers'. I commented on the sayings and the bits of wisdom that I wanted to convey, and I used the Rose Medallion to see the words of a poet of the future.

To use the Medallion, one must first look at the face side. The medallion is made of reddish clay and is about 3 inches wide. The face side has the image of a woman-the Goddess Inanna-one of the first Goddesses, a Sumerian Goddess, whose symbol was The Rose. After looking at the face side, I look at the blank side, and touch the Red Key. I don't always touch the Red Key, but it seems to help. The Red Key opens the doors to all of the altar rooms of all the religions, past, present, and future. It also unlocks all of the locks of the chains that bind you. After looking at the face side of the Medallion, I look at the blank side. Then, a story, a poem, lyrics to a song, or a saying, might appear on the blank side.

There was Magic that occurred during the speech, particularly at the end. I cannot comment on it. It was a surprise to me. A Phoenix symbol appeared-and other things happened. It was all a surprise, and also a shock to me-you must believe that. I think of it every day.

The story of that speech, and the planning of my trip to Eleusis, with my guardian, Panelle, and my counselor, Morain, has been documented elsewhere. All of the events leading up to the speech, the places I visited, the entertainment, the market, all of this has been described by others. Of the story of my childhood, my friends, Anka and Troyana, much has been written. There are many stories about one of my teachers, Pythagoras, and Vorios, the chief magician at the Temple, and others that share the life of the Temple with us. Looking back on it all, especially the speech, the events seemed to favor the Apollonian side of my Priestess-hood. I don't feel that there was all that much of the dark nature, the dark of humanity in the speech at Eleusis. It was a speech of renewal, I had been planning it for a long time, and it was meant to be uplifting-a reaching for the higher gates.

This book will relate my ideas about the dark side of human nature. Dionysus for me represents those qualities of the dark side-the drinking of the wine, the midnight revels, the madness- things that when taken further down to the lower gates, without control or moderation, can lead to all kinds of problems. I may or may not succeed here in offering my views through poetry, song lyrics, story, dreams, and sayings. In the end, the balance is what matters-

The balance of the dark and the light, The Sacred Masculine and Sacred Feminine-"The Union of Opposites". Also our reverence and connection with the Earth, the Four Directions, and Spirit must balance whatever is dark within us.

Prologue to Theoclea's book-'More Whispers'

2.

The KeyRose Reading

Theoclea rose from her desk and looked out the window once again. The birds were gone and a cloud obscured the moon. She took the KeyRose Box off of its' shelf and sat down once again at the writing desk in her chamber. She had the black lacquer box in her hand, and fondly touched the leather Red Key attached to the brass plate on the top of the box.

This box was specially crafted for her by the merchant that she had almost met once again at Eleusis, the one who made the special Goddess statues. She opened the box and placed all of the pieces inside on a black cloth on the desk. She smiled as she handled the thirty images, like seeing old friends. The images were on small gold-colored thick pieces of fine paper. The warm radiance of a crystal lantern illuminated the black cloth and the pieces. One by one she placed them on the right side of the cloth, making sure that all of the images could be seen. She left the blank pieces in the box.

She looked down at all of the familiar pieces on the right side of the cloth. *The Ancient Mother; the Drum; Music; the Dance; Balance; The Rose; The Guardian; The Bulls-eye; The Fingerprint; The Pentacle-Man; The Column;* and the other pieces. She also looked at the pieces that she had added to the original set that had been handed down to her- *The Storm Cloud; The Lightning flash; The Knife; the Red Key; The Rose Medallion; Magic in the Air,* and others.

She liked using the KeyRose because it allowed her to add images to the blank pieces, making this set her own personal set. Anka had her stones, Troyana had her cards, but Theoclea had been given the original KeyRose Box (The box of possibilities), and the Rose Medallion, as a part of her initiation when she became the Pythian Priestess, the Delphic Oracle. She turned on the musical chimes set that was powered by a crystal lantern. The tune that it played was composed by Pythagoras just for this purpose of using the KeyRose images in Meditation. Her hand slowly passed over the images. One of them seemed to be singing to her. It was *The Pentacle-Man*, a man with outstretched arms and legs within a circle. She placed it in the center of the cloth.

She looked at the other pieces. Was there another piece that was singing to her, or wanting to play with the first piece? Yes, there was-*The Rose*. She placed it below *The Pentacle-Man* on the center of the cloth. Was there another piece that beckoned, a piece that wanted to be with the others in the center of the cloth? Nothing came to her, so she let her hand do the picking, for the hand itself often knows which images to seek. Her hand picked two pieces, *The Fingerprint, and the Guardian of The Gate.* Most people had an aversion to the *Guardian* piece, seeing a soldier, but she imagined him as a Guardian of some kind. An odd combination, of pieces she thought briefly, as she looked at the pieces that had been chosen.

Her hand continued to travel over the pieces- *the Lightning Flash and the Storm Cloud* (two of her own pieces that she had added herself) felt warm to the touch, so she added them to the images in the center. Both pieces were on the cover of her 'Whispers' book. She looked at all of the pieces that she had placed in the center of the cloth. Usually four or five pieces at the most, called to her in a reading. It was unusual that so many pieces were in this reading. Something was still missing, yet she did not feel the need to add an image on a blank piece. The images were all there.

273

She looked at all of the images on the right and the *Ancient Mother* called to her. As she looked at the *Ancient Mother* and placed her in the center, she recalled the poem about this piece that had appeared to her on the Rose Medallion. She whispered the poem as the chimes rang.

ANCIENT MOTHER

Ancient Mother,
what do you see,
moon-lit mirth,
infinity?
The past, the future,
the shore at night,
All are part of your
luminous sight.
The verdant plain,
the lake of gloom,
the perfumed garden,
where roses bloom.
The risen sun,
the sunbeams' motes
the foam-born singer
with the sweet-scented notes?
Ancient mother, I hear your song,

274

a song of hope, for all day long
it calls to me-
when I'm alone,
the heart-gladdened-notes ,
From the incense-throne.
They speak of Eleusis

What a joyful scene
when Demeter the mother
met Proserpine
You sing of that joy,
you sing of that place,
you sing of a time when the Human Race
shall seize the thunder
and forget the shame
And sing joyful songs
that honor your name.
Ancient Mother
we hear your song
Calling all of us together
In a joyful throng.
Our voices will rise in a
candle-lit swoon,
And the sound will be heard
By the Stars and the Moon.

She placed the *Ancient Mother* with the other pieces in the center. Of all of the pieces she loved this one the most. Another piece called to her, the *Large Shell*, and she placed it near the Ancient Mother. It reminded her of a sandy beach near the sea. Next, she had to pick the piece that she would never choose. As usual, she picked *The Rigid Structure*, the piece with the dot on the inside of a rectangular structure. Something about this piece had never appealed to her. She placed this piece on the left side of the cloth.

Theoclea then closed her eyes and visually looked at the remaining pieces in her mind. They floated about, falling here and there like snowflakes falling through a cloud of whispers. The chimes gently played. She opened her eyes and looked at the remaining pieces on the right side of the cloth. Quickly she turned them all over so that she could not see the image sides.

She then placed her hand on the Pentacle and Rose that Pythagoras had given to her. It looked like an ordinary gold-colored basket with a black metal star in it. The symbols of Apollo and Dionysus joined together to form a Pentacle. The light and the dark joined, and yet, the four Roses at four of the inside points hinted at the presence of Goddesses bringing a kind of balance to the Symbol.

Theoclea's personal Pentacle and Rose was highly charged. The Dragon whose breath seeped up into the chamber under the Tripod Chair had finally told her a secret. The Pentacle and Rose had to be charged once in a while in order to keep working. The charging was done in a secret ritual.

Theoclea placed her hand in the center of the star and felt its' power surging through her. She then took her hand and placed it over the remaining pieces on the right that had all been turned over. Two of the pieces felt warm to her touch. Usually, one piece was being offered to her, one random piece from the Macrocosm, or Universe. Today, two pieces felt warm to her touch. She picked up both pieces, and slowly, one by one she turned them over.

The first piece was the *Red Key*. She hesitated before she turned over the remaining piece, the last piece. She heard a voice in her mind "it's starting, It's Starting, IT"S STARTING!" She held the remaining piece in her hand and then turned it over. It was the *Rose Medallion*, The Token of Inanna, one the pieces that she had personally added to the set. The Pentacle and the Rose and the KeyRose (The box of possibilities) had spoken.

She put the pieces back in the Black Lacquer box, and put the cloth away. The box was put back in its' special place on a shelf. She touched the crystal lantern and the light dimmed and went off. Briefly she wondered about what made the lanterns work-some kind of lost magic, she had always assumed, the wisdom of the past that had somehow been lost. She lay down on her bed, and sleep quickly enveloped her. Her cat, "Kitty" was nestled against her. Kitty stood up and arched her back. Suddenly she looked about as if someone else was in the room. After a minute of walking around, satisfied that no one else was there, she jumped back on the bed, and fell asleep against Theoclea.

Addendum three

I offer for your reading pleasure-
The first chapter of
The first story
In the 'Whispers' book-
The story is
called 'The Others'
In the story you will meet
Ernest Shackleton, the
explorer of the Antarctic,
and see how his life might have been
affected by meeting
Pythagoras, Theoclea,
and 'The Others'.

Chapter One...The Dreams

"Whispers, first I heard the whispers. I was both outside and inside. I felt cold, bitter cold, then I was sitting at a desk. I looked about the room. There was a feeling, a feeling like I'd been somewhere outside for the last few days, walking, walking with three men who were at the very edge of their endurance. They were frost-bitten and hungry, and were walking on icy, mountainous terrain. I was walking with them. I seemed to be in two places, with them, and at a desk. I was wearing white. Some of the items in the room were recognizable, some were not. There was a lantern on the desk, but it was not a crystal lantern. There was a flame and a knob. I turned the knob and the flame went out. I looked around the room and saw some objects that seemed to be the tools of fishermen. There were nets, knives, ropes, and the like. The wind was howling outside, and the men's frost-bitten legs kept walking,

walking. Their souls had experienced a dark night that had gone on for months and months. I was with them, but they couldn't see me, of course."

" One of them was the leader of the others. I seemed to be able to read the leader's mind to some extent. There was disappointment at not achieving a goal, but in the failure, there was the possibility of something else that had happened, something unexpected. 'If only we can get there,' he seemed to be saying. 'If only we can keep going. All of the men left behind must be rescued.' I also sensed that he had a secret. He had found something. I looked into his memories further, and I saw ice, and other men, bitter cold, freezing rain, and their boat being broken to bits by the ice that has encased it. The rest was icy whiteness. That's the dream, Theoclea."

Theoclea turned her head toward the window. It was a bright, warm sunny spring day outside. A flock of geese flew across the sky. She then looked back at Pythagoras:

"You've never mentioned anything to me before about your dreams, Pythagoras."

"I don't seem to dream a lot, but during my visit here, at Delphi, I seem to be having dreams, and remembering more and more about them."

Pythagoras thought for a few seconds.

"I was in a room. There was a book on a desk, and it seemed to be turned to a certain page. At the top of the page were words in a language that I was familiar with in the dream. The words said 'Grytviken Whaling Station', Stromness."

"Is there such a place?" Theoclea asked.

"Not that I know of, but I'm not a sailor or a fisherman" replied Pythagoras. "Oh yes, there was a brown box and it had a wire attached to it. I heard a voice coming from the box, just a few words, here and there amongst crackling noises. I heard a name, 'Jacobsen', coming from the box, and knew that it was my name in the dream. I heard the words "South Georgia Island' coming from the box. There was also a lamp on the desk with a wire attached to it as well, and the light coming from it was not the kind of light that we get from the crystal lanterns."

"I have seen talking boxes, and lamps with wires, or cords attached to them in my dreams and visions of the future," Theoclea said. "I suspect that there will be other dreams-keep a journal by your bedside."

A few days later Theoclea summoned Pythagoras. She was in the South Arbor admiring the trees.

"Pythagoras, I've had a dream as well that seems to be related to yours. In the dream I was in a room.

I saw a brown box on a table, and music was coming from it. There was a window, and I walked over to it. Outside I saw that it was snowing, there seemed to be a teaming seaport, with many ships, men, and cargo being loaded. The room was not the simple room in your dream. There was something elegant about the room. I heard a moaning sound behind me. Up until that time in the dream, I knew that I was in a dream or vision, but suddenly I was there, and I saw a man lying on the floor. He was dying, and clutching his chest. I was dressed in white, and bent over him. I touched his chest and felt that his heart had stopped beating. I placed my hands on him, and concentrated sharing my aura with his, and his heart started beating again! I realized that his heart was damaged from years of hard living, perhaps from drinking, or habitually putting himself in perilous situations. I did what I could for him."

"He came to, and gradually he stood up. He was dazed. He looked around the room. He seemed to stop and gaze directly in my direction, then continued to look around the room. I could read his memories, and saw the same scene that you saw, I saw him with two other men walking, painfully over snow topped mountainous terrain, I sensed that there was someone else with them, a Spirit, perhaps. For a moment, I saw that the Spirit was you, Pythagoras! I then saw that they walked down a mountainside and there was a wooden sign post. The sign said 'South Georgia, Grytviken'. All of this I got from being able to search his memories while he was recovering from heart failure in that room. I sensed that he was the same man who was the leader of the others in your dream, Pythagoras."

"In my dream, Theoclea continued, "he staggered over to a desk, sat down, and started to write in a Journal. He wrote one word 'Tromso'. Then he wrote 'Lady in White, Healer'. He put down a date, but the day was smudged. I could only see the year, it was 1918. He then went to a large box with latches that was over in a corner, opened it and took something out."

"What was it?" Pythagoras asked.

"It was a crystal lantern," Theoclea replied. "He placed the crystal lantern on the desk, and then started to look for something else in the case. He finally found what he was looking for, and brought it out."

"What did he bring out?" Pythagoras asked.

"It was a Rose Medallion, with the face of a woman. She looked like Axcelotl-with a crown of crystals."

"The lost medallion!" Pythagoras shouted. "He found it!"

"Yes, Pythagoras, he found it. We must remember, though that I can only intervene like that once in a person's life-heal the mortally wounded-even stop death. I suspect that Axcelotl could do more. By the way, Pythagoras, I had the distinct impression that this man had not only found the medallion, but had already met with Axcelotl and the two others, and not just once, but twice!"

Addendum Four

The first two chapters of the 'Dracula' story from the book-
'Phoebe (The Delphic Oracle) meets Dracula (The Vampire)'
In other stories in this book-
A new Oracle-Phoebe, meets Nikola Tesla, and shows him the oldest city in the Americas- Caral, Peru-
Phoebe's friends intervene in 'The Miracle at the OK Corral'.
Theoclea watches Bix, a jazz musician from the 1920's, and helps him to cross the 'Final Gate'.

...and we witness in the final story, the reunion of Theoclea, Morain and Panelle!
Check out our website-
www.panorpheus.com

Chapter One...The Four Meet

Phoebe sat with the others, deep in meditation. It was the beginning of the year. They had all inhaled the sacred powder, and one by one, they came back to awareness- the bone inhalers lay on the ground in front of them.

Phoebe was the first to speak:

"This business of the 'Evil Ones', the 'Conchus' must stop.

Potavi concurred with a nod and a simple "Yes." She was, as usual, wearing the magical henna on her hands and feet, the rest of her was heavily tattooed, so that her hands and feet seemed to be invisible.

Tatavis, sitting in her wheeled chair offered her opinion.

"We have had peace in Caral for so long, that it is shocking to feel it amongst us again. I thought that evil was a thing of the past for us. My being confined to this chair was the result of an evil act by a madman. He was tried and sentenced, and order was restored to the city. Then it flared up again, and Phoebe came to our city to stop it. Since then, we've had Peace, *and Phoebe has prophesied a millennium of Peace. She has also made the Prophecy that Caral would be known as the 'Purple City', and that the Spirit of Tradition would appear, and be with us, but these things have yet to be."*

Phoebe replied, "I talked of a millennium of Peace, but did not say that there would not be acts of evil here and there, evil is always amongst us. "It's like the old, sad songs that we play on the pelican bone flutes. The melodies remain in our minds-they don't go away. Evil is like that, 'it won't go away-we must hold it at bay', as the old saying goes. We must be eternally vigilant, and exercise control over it. It's an ancient problem. We just have to be prepared and guard against it. The problem of these... creatures, the 'conchus' sucking the blood of our sleeping young may be a new problem for us, but it is an old problem, it has appeared in other cultures. In Greece they were called 'empusa', or 'lamia', horrible winged demon-women who attacked youths to suck out their blood and eat their flesh. The story comes from an account of Lamia, a child of Zeus, who was driven insane by Zeus's jealous wife, Hera. She then killed her own children, and then went about attacking human children, taking their blood and eating them out of hatred and revenge. I made other prophecies too... You're right, Tatavis, I predicted that Caral would be known as 'The Purple City', and this, has not come true... yet. "

Phalanx replied: "All of this talk of blood is making me sick. I'll take my ceremonial bow and arrows, stand guard over

290

the city, and one by one I'll shoot them down! Phoebe-why not send your crows out at night to hunt them and eat them!"

Phoebe thought for a moment, and then said,

"It's not as easy as that, these creatures are not alive, they are already dead, a kind of 'undead', walking or flying amongst us in the night. There is a procedure that must be followed for killing them. Unfortunately I don't know what it is. My Medallion, the Medallion of Gaia has been of no help, either in this matter. I stare at the face of Gaia on the front, and then look at the back of the medallion-usually words or pictures appear that help me with my prophecies and meditations-I keep seeing these words-

*'Nothing is ever destroyed.
Everything comes back
in endless recreations,
and reincarnations.'*

She looked at the rose-colored medallion with the face of Gaia that she always wore around her neck for these meetings of 'The Four', as she called them. She reached over for the bone inhaler, put some powder into it, then put it down.

"As for the crows-they have very definite tastes when it comes to hunting and eating, and the 'conchus' are definitely not on their list. The answer to this problem might be simple, it

might be right under our noses- we just can't see it. It might be right here!"

"Why talk of the past, or the present?" All eyes were on Potavi, who had been sitting quietly, listening to the others. Potavi was a woman from the lands north of Peru, who had recently joined their circle. She was a healer.

"The future is where the answer lies-the far future, perhaps. Phoebe, you can travel into the future as well as the past and appear in human form, am I right?"

"Yes, Potavi, but it is not really a human form, and it certainly has nothing to do with the 'Conchus'!"Phoebe reached for the bone inhaler, and inhaled the Sacred Dust.

"No, Phoebe, I wasn't implying anything. I was just offering the opinion that you may have to travel into the future or the past, find the solution or intervene at some point!" She looked in the gold-colored bag that she always carried around her waist. "Yes, here it is"-she took out a calling card, and handed it to Phoebe." I would see these people, they may have the solution to the problem."

Phoebe coughed a little, then looked at the card 'The Antiquarian Brotherhood' it said in bold type, then, there was what appeared to Phoebe to be an address, and a communication number. "Where and When shall I have to travel to, so that I can meet these people?"

You must travel to the year 2267 in Future Time, to the city of Cairo, in Egypt," Potavi replied.

"You will be meeting the head of the Brotherhood-Dracula, I believe is his name."

"The name sounds familiar to me-I shall have to do some research, but I'll go at once!"

Chapter Two... The Board Room

He swiveled around in his armchair, and stared out the balcony doors. He was in the Board Room on the twelfth floor, and the view was spectacular. To the left he saw the Giza plateau, the Pyramids and the Sphinx. He looked to his right and slowly surveyed the scene, a rich sunset of red, orange and purple hues backlighted the scene of modern Cairo in the twenty-third century. As his gaze slowly turned to the right, he saw huge skyscrapers, amidst older buildings. A wireless electrical transmission tower loomed in the distance. He thought of Nikola Tesla, the man whose ideas made the towers possible.

It had been three years since the unexpected visit of 'The Star Children', Abderus and Alcena, the son and daughter of Theoclea, the Delphic Oracle and Pythagoras. The children alerted 'The Brotherhood' that the Corporation had been doing business with an unsavory character, a magician in ancient Egypt, named Morvan. Shortly after that, Morvan met his end. In the interim, 'The Antiquarian Brotherhood, or Corporation, had continued to do a brisk business of trading precious antiques and artifacts through time, to and from many places on the Earth. They had been in business for well over a thousand years, and were generally very careful about who they did business with. They had just concluded a deal in which they had sent a rare Leland-Arnaud talking machine, one of the first of its' kind from the twentieth century back to the fourteenth century to a rich alchemist, and in return, they had received a rare tapestry from the castle of Prince Vlad, depicting the impalement of a nobleman. Things like that were definitely distasteful to him, but business was business, and he was acquiring the tapestry for a wealthy man who had, shall we say, unusual tastes. The business of the day had concluded, and he had taken down the crystal triangle of protection, and put the crystals back on their shelf. He lifted his glass of wine, ate a piece of cheese, followed it with a slice of sausage, and kicked back in the chair as the sunset quietly disappeared and the night returned. He thought of the others in the past, who could not see the sunset.

His associates all called him 'The Boss', rarely using his real name. He opened the balcony door and a bat flew into the board room, circled around and landed on his shoulder-he picked up a piece of the sausage, and fed it to the bat, for this particular bat had acquired a taste for the unusual.

'The Boss' liked the night. He looked out at the skyline and saw other bats flying across the full moon, and smiled. He felt like watching an old movie tonight, perhaps a classic from the twentieth century, 'Dracula', with Bela Lugosi. Several of his associates had remarked on his close resemblance to Lugosi, and at parties, he sometimes feigned Lugosi's foreign accent, and quoted lines from the film. Well, he was 'The Boss', and could do as he pleased. Around the board room one could see only a small part of his collection of items from the late nineteenth and twentieth century that had anything to do with Dracula. There were framed ticket stubs from the 1927 play that enjoyed a long run in New York. On one wall there was a framed poster from the 1931 film 'Dracula' with Lugosi, of course in the leading role. There were a few other things, here and there.

Suddenly, a gust of wind entered the room...he had forgotten to close the balcony door. As he walked over to close the door, he suddenly had the strange feeling that someone was staring at him, He gazed at the night sky, and saw a flock of crows crossing the moon. Closing the balcony door, he drew the red drapes, but was still troubled by an uncomfortable feeling. Then, he turned around and to his amazement, saw a woman standing behind him. She was dressed in red, black and gold, very fashionably dressed, obviously the clothes were one of a kind, made by a top designer, probably from London or Paris. A crow sat on her shoulder. "May I?" she gestured at the cheese plate. "Yes,...of course," he said. She took two pieces of the cheese, ate one, and then gave the other one to the crow. Obviously, this was not an ordinary crow, the crow had acquired unusual tastes. She looked at him carefully.

'The Boss' continued to gaze at her, she seemed to be in her mid-thirties, and had long beautiful red hair. She looked about the room, and saw the movie poster.

"Perhaps, you would like some sausage and a glass of wine," he said, still wondering how she had gotten into the room.

"Yes," she replied, "I'm famished." He went over and lifted the wine bottle, poured her a glass, refilled his own, and offered her the sausage plate.

298

"Well," he said, "since we seem to be dining together tonight, I think that introductions are in order, I am usually called 'The Boss' by my associates."

"You can't kid me," she said, "I know that you're Dracula," she replied. He was astounded and almost dropped his wine glass. When he had regained his composure, he said, "…and who might you be?"

"I am Phoebe, The Delphic Oracle, the Third to hold The Seat of Prophecy, and I have something that we must discuss as soon as possible!!"

Addendum Five

**The first two chapters
From a forthcoming book-**

**'Phoebe
(The Delphic Oracle)
in
The Medallion
Of Gaia'**

Chapter One... The Temple of Delphi-Greece...ca. 500 B.C.

Theoclea opened her eyes and gazed at the others. They sat on comfortable cushions in an anteroom of the Temple of Delphi-Theoclea, The Delphic Oracle, Pythagoras, and their children-the twins-'The Star Children', as they were sometimes called by the residents of the Temple. Theoclea wore the violet robe that had been given to her by the guardian of the third gate that had appeared beside the pond, in Egypt. She also wore the Red Key and The Rose Medallion. In the room, one large window let in a great deal of light and the room was bright. Outside a flight of crows could be seen, flying east, followed by a white pigeon.

They had all been meditating to soft chimes that played on a crystal-powered music player like the kind that was used

301

on Atlantis. The player was like the crystal lanterns that lit part of the Temple of Delphi... a relic from a distant past, something that simply worked, without their knowing the technology behind the workings- a lost magic, perhaps. Pythagoras and the children had awakened from their meditation before Theoclea. The children were dressed in simple white tunics, with gold braided ropes for belts. Alcena was the first to speak after the meditation ended and the chimes stopped playing.

"Theoclea, tell us a story!"

"What kind of a story do you want to hear?" she asked Alcena.

"A story about a mystery of the future... perhaps a story that you have seen on your Rose Medallion, or a story that came from a KeyRose reading!"

"A story about," Abderus turned to Pythagoras, "what was that word Pythagoras, that you used to describe people of the future who solve mysteries?"

"Detectives!" Pythagoras said, smiling at the children. He wore a white tunic also, but hanging from a red corded belt was an ornate ceremonial dagger. Several family meetings of this kind had been held, and they had all been to Egypt, and experienced adventure and mystery there. Storytelling was a part of their get-togethers, and because Theoclea considered the right words at the right time to be among her many gifts, she had proven to be the best storyteller.

"Ah," she replied. "So you want to hear a story about a detective and a mystery of the future?"

"Yes, said Abderus, "and can the story have the Muhajihadeem in it too?"

She thought for a moment. "So, you want assassins-Muhajihadeem in the story as well!"

"How about a story that includes a mysterious search for a rare object," Alcena said, "like the book that we found with Pythagoras and Vorios during our adventure in Egypt!"

"...and how 'bout you include yourself, Theoclea, and Pythagoras.

"Morain, your counselor. and Panelle, your guardian could be in it as well!!"

Theoclea glanced at Pythagoras.

"Well, there will be someone named Pythagoras, but he won't be the Pythagoras that we know!" Theoclea replied.

Pythagoras knew the story and decided to have some fun with Theoclea.

"Theoclea, can you include a fantastic city of the future, in an exotic strange location, with structures in it that are based on...geometric principles. Can you also include strange music and dance as well?"

Theoclea's eyes glanced up at the ceiling and she sighed.

'He had to say that,' she thought.

"Yes, okay, I'll tell you a story about the greatest detective of all time, and the search for a rare object!"

"The story will need a villain,"Alcena said.

"Why do the villains always have to be men, how 'bout a woman. There are hardly any women villains in our stories,"Abderus said.

"So, you want a woman as the villain...yes, I know who that would be!" Theoclea said.

Alcena, thought for a moment and said, "It would be a great mystery if it had a mechanical man from the future, and part of took place way out in outer space, and way in the future. You've told us that you've seen these things in your visions and dreams. It may take more than a few meetings to tell the whole story!"

Theoclea looked over at Pythagoras, he looked down, then met Theoclea's gaze, and tears welled up in both of his eyes. She smiled and nodded toward him.

She closed her eyes, thought for a few moments, and then opened them.

Theoclea said, "Yes, I know just the one! A story that will fit all of your expectations...and more!"

"The Medallion of Gaia! You know, of course, the names of the first Three Oracles, don't you? Gaia, Themis, and Phoebe-but do you know that a Medallion was made for Gaia, and then passed on to Themis, when she became the Oracle? Then

it was passed on to Phoebe, who eventually became the Oracle of Caral Peru...but that's another story. Then, the Medallion of Gaia was lost or stolen! That's yet another story in itself! The Medallion of Gaia was made of red clay, like the Rose Medallion that I wear. It was said to be the most powerful medallion, more powerful than all of the others combined. The name of the maker of the first medallion is shrouded in the mystery of the past!"

"It may have been made on the continent of Lemuria that preceded Atlantis!" Theoclea said. She then showed them her medallion, The Medallion of Inanna, with the face of Inanna on the front side, and once again described its' use. She wore the Red Key and reminded the children of what the keys stood for.

"There are two things that I must mention here," she said." It is important for you to remember that the original Gods and Goddesses of Greece were called 'The Titans'.

"Also, we often use the phrase-'As above, so below', without having any insight into the many layers of meaning that may be implied. This story may give you some clues to think about."

"Let me tell you about the detective."

"First of all, I must say that even though our detective is to be the greatest detective of the future-I would describe him as a wearer of the black key. My Rose Medallion told me that. Many people say that children are born with the gold key-and the medallion told me that he never really had the gold key, that his

305

childhood was lacking…in certain respects, and he received the black key and a wound early on. That would account for his sarcastic nature, his habit of treating people harshly at times, his abrupt, scornful way with women, his fits of temper, and that mysterious snarl and half smile that he presented-curling up his left upper lip and revealing his teeth. He also smoked cigarettes, and sometimes drank fermented liquids that were much stronger than wine. He had a slight speech impediment, a slight lisp that added to his dark sardonic nature. He only fired a gun when he absolutely had to, and used his wits and his fists well. Women were very attracted to him. Detectives at that time, often referred to themselves as 'Private Eyes'"

"During the time in the future that he is to be born into, all of the medallions have been found, at one time or another, except for the first…the medallion of Gaia. How the medallion was lost shall remain a Mystery. Also, I must tell you that before the Temple of Delphi was dedicated to Apollo, The Temple was devoted to Hestia, the Goddess of the hearth. That is why the cracks in the earth where the dragon's breath seeps up under the tripod chair are called "The Hearth at the Navel of the Earth'.

Now, through sources that I cannot reveal, because they are associated with the other realms, I was made aware in a vision, of the possible existence of the Gaia Medallion-about 3000 years in the future, on a continent that we know nothing about now, but will be called 'North America'. I was told that the medallion would finally be somewhere on that continent, and I was made aware of the skillful work of our detective, who was well known in the City of San Francisco.

Obviously, I needed someone familiar with the medallion, someone with a passion for finding it-Someone who could match wits with the detective, smoke a cigarette now and then, and who was just as abrupt in her manner as he was. I needed a woman of great power, who, if need be, could summon the forces of thousands, perhaps millions of crows, and could call the spirits of Eternal Vigilance, Sonja, Aura, and Axcelotl! A woman who would know the location of the second Oracle-Themis! The choice was obvious- I needed the help of Phoebe-the Third Oracle to hold the Seat of Prophecy-'The Bright and Shining One'. "

"What's a cigarette?" Alcena said...

"Theoclea...I know you've told us this before...but, what exactly is a ...gun?" Abderus said.

"Why don't you take your teardrops
One by one before you hesitate
Dry them all out in the sun
Before it gets to late…"
Lyrics to the song 'Sunshine', performed by
The Paul Whiteman band with
Bing Crosby
and Bix Beiderbecke
recorded by the Leland-Arnaud
Talking Machine Co. ca. mid 1920's

Chapter Two...
Phoebe in San
Francisco

Phoebe blinked her eyes a few times to get used to the brightness of the sun. She walked briskly down the city street, noticing that some of the facades of the buildings had ornate ironwork-something that she had not seen since her time in London and New York watching Tesla. She paused to look at a car. It was a 1949 Buick Roadmaster. She knew that because there were four ventiports on the side panel below the hood, and about a foot below them was the name 'Roadmaster'. There were whitewall tires, and the tire hubcaps said 'Buick'. She walked around to the front of the car. It had something called a 'twenty-five tooth dollar grin grille, sometimes called a 'bucktooth grille', and the top of the grille said 'Buick Eight' in bold black letters. On the top of the hood was the famous Buick 'Gunsight' hood ornament. She walked around to the back of the car and looked at the back trunk latch. The latch was silver-colored chrome, with red inserts that had the words 'Dyna Flow' boldly shown in gold. 'Very nice, the colors of the Delphic Oracle-red black and gold, with silver thrown in,' she thought. She had never been to the 1950's, and knew that the cars of the late forties and fifties had flashy chrome grilles, hood ornaments, whitewall tires, and more.

She moved on and looked at the buildings. What an odd mix in this city–Art Nouveau, Art Deco, Modern, and Victorian designs on stone, wood, brick, and iron. Looking up at the sky she saw the crows, and over the tops of the buildings she could make out parts of the Golden Gate Bridge. She was dressed in red, black and gold, of course, and the style was in keeping with the latest fashion of London, Paris and New York. Theoclea had told her that she was the only one who could pull this off, and she was right. She reached into a pocket of the long black coat that she was wearing, pulled out a silver cigarette case, and turned it over several times, its mirrored surface gleamed in the sunlight. She opened it, took out a cigarette, closed the case and reached for a lighter in another pocket. She lit the cigarette, and inhaled the smoke, coughing a few times. She had not tried a cigarette since the night that she and Tesla had dined at Delmonico's. She tossed the cigarette down and ground it out with her shoe.

'Well, that's what people in his city, at this time do to enjoy themselves', she thought, although she didn't get it. It was nothing like the 'Sacred Dust', the white powder that she had in another pocket, along with a bone inhaler, from her city-Caral, Peru. One could use them to go into trance, to meditate-to create magic. She was Phoebe, the Oracle of Caral, Peru, and had travelled over a thousand miles north, and five thousand years in the future to start this intervention.

People all around her were walking past her, and all seemed to be walking in the opposite direction that she was going in. Nobody noticed her. She was suddenly relieved to see that the crows seemed to be settling in on a building in the next block. She hurriedly walked across the intersection, took out the card in her pocket, read the name 'Sam Diamond, Private Eye'. She looked at the address on the card and knew that she was heading toward the building that the crows had settled on. There were hundreds of them, and they were with her. When she arrived at the entrance, she stood before an ironwork gate. She liked gates, they meant 'change' in her mind. The crows looked down, staring at her. They

311

were one mind, one entity, waiting for her commands. One of the crows flew down and perched on her shoulder. She reached into her pocket and took out some bread crumbs and fed it, all of a sudden the crow flew up and rejoined the others. She noticed that were also three amorphous lights hovering over the doorway.

Without warning, she was quickly aware of something else, she turned around and saw him, across the street, leaning against a tree reading a newspaper, wearing a light brown trench coat, and a stylish brown hat. Carefully, he folded up the newspaper, placed it under his arm, and stared directly at Phoebe, his unblinking eyes taking in everything, the crows, the lights, everything. She nodded slightly at him. He nodded back- 'The Reporter' she thought. Phoebe was then aware that to the right of him, about thirty feet away, there seemed to be a woman, also leaning against a tree, and she was looking at Phoebe. She was dressed in a stylish black coat, and wore a large black hat, and on her shoulder there was a hooded black falcon. The woman closed her eyes, and took an unusually long blink, then she looked away, lit a cigarette, and blew a smoke ring up toward the lowest leaves of the tree, and tossed the match. The falcon remained perched on her shoulder. She turned once again, and looked at Phoebe scornfully.

Phoebe stared at her with a worried look on her face. She looked back at the man, and he too was staring at the woman, who didn't seem to acknowledge his presence. Phoebe quickly glanced from one to the other. The woman looked away from Phoebe, and stared into space, as if preoccupied with something else. Then there was another long blink. Phoebe turned around-she had seen enough.

She walked up to the front door of the building, walked in, and saw that there were buttons lined up on a wall. One of the buttons said. 'Sam Diamond, Private Eye' in bold black letters. She pushed the button, and the door buzzed-she opened it and went in. There was an elevator, and she took it to the third floor. The address on the card said office 303. When the elevator stopped at the third floor, she walked out, and quickly found office 303, turned the door handle and walked in. A blonde secretary was sitting at a desk. She walked over, and the secretary glanced up, smiled and reached out her hand.

"I'm Edie, Mr. Diamond's Secretary, and you are?"

"Phoebe Bright, I believe that I have an appointment."

Edie quickly looked her up and down, approvingly.

"Yes, of course, I'll let him know that you're here."

Edie walked over to a door that said 'Sam Diamond', and walked through.

"Phoebe Bright is here to see you Sam, she has an appointment-and she's a real knockout- a redhead-looks to be in her late thirties-maybe early forties."

He smiled a half smile that almost looked like a snarl, took out a pouch of tobacco, laid out a packet of cigarette papers, and said,

"Well what are you waiting for, precious, send her in."

Down on the street, the woman had disappeared. The man turned to his right and walked half a block.

He said something to no one in particular-

"Did you get that feed, Captain, were the zooms and close-ups clear?"

A voice in his mind said-

"Yes, it was all clear except for the other woman, she was partially blocked by a tree. Who was she?"

"It was Livia, and the falcon," he replied.

There was a pause.

"That complicates things," the voice in his mind said.

"We're going to bring you back."

In an instant, he simply disappeared.